UNITED HEROES

UNITED HEROES

THIRTY LEGENDARY REDS AND THEIR INCREDIBLE STORIES

Reach Sport

UNITED HEROES

Copyright © Manchester United Football Club

The right of Manchester United Football Club to be identified as the owner of this work has been asserted in accordance with the Copyright, Designs and Patents Act, 1988. All rights reserved. No part of this publication may be reproduced, stored in a retrieval system, or transmitted in any form, or by any means – electronic, mechanical, photocopying, recording or otherwise – without the prior permission in writing of the copyright holders, nor be otherwise circulated in any form of binding or cover other than in which it is published and without a similar condition being imposed on the subsequent publisher.

Hardback edition first published in Great Britain in 2024.

reachsport.com   @reach_sport

Reach Sport is a part of Reach PLC Ltd, 5 St Paul's Square, Liverpool, L3 9SJ
One Canada Square, Canary Wharf, London, E15 5AP

ISBN: 9781916811195

Illustrations: Stanley Chow
Editor: Paul Davies
Words: Steve Bartram, Joe Ganley, Charlie Ghagan,
Ian McLeish, Harry Robinson, Isaac Stronge
Designer: Chris Collins
Production editor: Adam Oldfield
Thanks to: Ben Ashby, Mark Froggatt, Ian Nolan

Photographic acknowledgements:
Mirrorpix, Getty Images, Alamy

Printed and bound by Buxton Press

CONTENTS

07	**Introduction**
08-13	David Beckham
14-19	George Best
20-25	Sir Matt Busby
26-31	Eric Cantona
32-37	Michael Carrick
38-43	Sir Bobby Charlton
44-49	Mary Earps
50-55	Duncan Edwards
56-61	Rio Ferdinand
62-67	Sir Alex Ferguson
68-73	Bruno Fernandes
74-79	Bill Foulkes
80-85	Ryan Giggs
86-91	Mark Hughes
92-97	Denis Irwin
98-103	Roy Keane
104-109	Denis Law
110-115	Billy Meredith
116-121	Gary Neville
122-127	Marcus Rashford
128-133	Bryan Robson
134-139	Wayne Rooney
140-145	Cristiano Ronaldo
146-151	Jack Rowley
152-157	Peter Schmeichel
158-163	Paul Scholes
164-169	Nobby Stiles
170-175	Ella Toone
176-181	Edwin van der Sar
182-187	Norman Whiteside

Hi there!

My name is Fred and I'm the Manchester United mascot. You may have spotted me on the Old Trafford pitch at home matches, where my job is to meet young supporters like you and to help cheer the team on to victory!

This brilliant book picks out 30 United heroes from the Reds' past and present, and includes plenty of names you will know well, like David Beckham and Cristiano Ronaldo, but also some your parents and grandparents will be able to tell you about.

Across the next 180 pages you'll learn all about some of the most important players and managers from United's proud history — from both the men's and women's teams. There are four Ballon d'Or winners, many record-breaking players, and some of the biggest names to ever kick a football.

As well as telling their amazing stories, I've also picked out some of the best stats about them.

Happy reading — and Glory, Glory Man United!

Fred the Red

'BECKS' DAVID BECKHAM

How a brilliantly talented lad from East London became a Reds legend and global superstar, with so many amazing goals and free-kicks along the way…

If ever there was someone who was born to be a United legend, it was the one and only David Beckham. His dad Ted was – and still is! – a massive Reds fan and gave his first son David the middle name Robert, after his all-time favourite player, Bobby Charlton. Young Becks grew up to idolise Sir Bobby too, and one of his earliest breaks in football was at the Bobby Charlton Soccer School, which Becks attended and even had his photo taken with the legend!

Despite coming from London, the Beckhams used to travel north to Old Trafford to watch United all the time, and Becks was even a mascot at a match at Old Trafford when he was just 11! Talk about a lifelong connection to Manchester United Football Club…

When he was a teenager, Becks played at Tottenham's school of excellence. Spurs would've loved to have signed him, but he only wanted to play for United!

Becks was voted the Sir Matt Busby Player of the Year by United fans in 1996/97.

David came second behind Brazilian Rivaldo in the Ballon d'Or voting in 1999.

The Reds weren't the only club he played for in England! For a short while in 1995 he played for Preston North End, on loan from United.

DAVID BECKHAM

Becks always worked hard for the Reds, and as well as crossing for others to score, he was a wonderful free-kick taker.

Becks's dreams came true when he signed schoolboy forms with United on his 14th birthday. It wasn't long before he became mates with a bunch of young trainee players who would go on to make history together. Lads like Gary and Phil Neville, Paul Scholes and Nicky Butt, plus the slightly older Ryan Giggs, these youngsters came through the ranks together, and many of them won the Youth Cup with United in 1992, becoming known for evermore as the Class of '92.

Manager Alex Ferguson knew he couldn't keep them out of the first team for long, and to the surprise of many United fans, Fergie sold established stars like Paul Ince and Andrei Kanchelskis to make way for Becks and co. Having made his senior debut in 1992, Beckham properly broke into the first team in the 1995/96 season and it didn't go too badly... he won both the Premier League and the FA Cup! And if he thought that was amazing, it was about to get even better. On the opening

DAVID BECKHAM

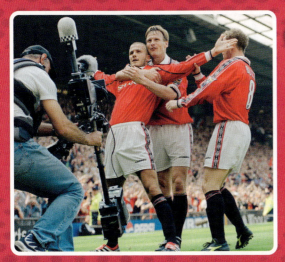

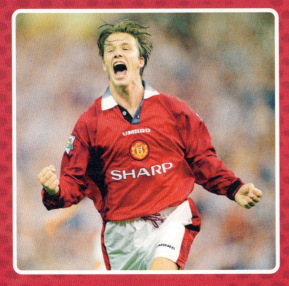

FRED'S FACTS!

394
Becks was only six games short of reaching 400 for United – something only 28 Reds have done in our history.

85
Beckham's United goals tally – not bad for a midfielder! The most he got in one season was 16 (2001/02).

115
Number of England caps he won – that's even more than Sir Bobby! Becks got 17 goals for his country.

day of the 1996/97 league season, he scored a goal from the halfway line against Wimbledon that is considered one of the greatest goals ever in England, and made the 21-year-old an overnight superstar. Becks was voted Young Player of the Year by his fellow footballers and a second Premier League medal followed for him at the end of that season.

DAVID BECKHAM

MAGIC MOMENT

It might have been his 53rd United appearance, but Becks made his true United breakthrough as a star player when he scored from the halfway line against Wimbledon in the first game of 1996/97. The goal was shown everywhere and suddenly the whole world knew his name!

A shock was to follow the next season when a brilliant Arsenal team pipped United to the title, but that only made Ferguson, Beckham and co fired up to reclaim our crown. And what was to follow was the greatest season in English football history... 1998/99 – the Treble!

This came on the back of a nightmare when our Dave was sent off for England against Argentina in the 1998 World Cup, making him public enemy no.1 in the eyes of many opposition fans, but it didn't stop him having the season of his life. We won the league in the last game against Spurs – Becks scoring United's first goal in the match – and in the Champions League final against Bayern Munich, he took the two corners that led to our dramatic injury-time goals. Unbelievable! By this point Becks was the most famous

DAVID BECKHAM

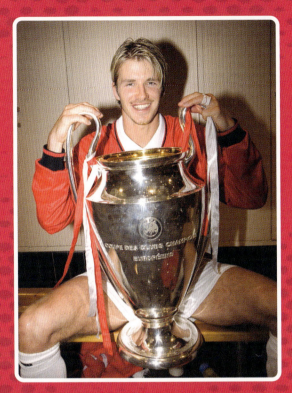

footballer in the world – and his celebrity grew thanks to his marriage to Spice Girl Victoria – but he didn't let his fame affect his game. He won the league with United again in 2000 and 2001, but by the time the 2002/03 season came round, his father-and-son-like relationship with Sir Alex was experiencing difficulties.

A move away from United looked likely, and so it turned out, but he went out on a high, winning a sixth and final Premier League title, and scoring a trademark brilliant free-kick in his final game for the Reds, away to Everton. He signed for Real Madrid and became a '*galactico*', and later played for LA Galaxy, AC Milan and Paris Saint-Germain, making the final appearance of his playing career for PSG in 2013, almost 10 years after leaving United. Thanks for the memories, Becks!

x6
Premier League: 1995/96, 1996/97, 1998/99, 1999/2000, 2000/01, 2002/03

x1
Champions League: 1999

x2
FA Cup: 1996, 1999

x2
Charity Shield: 1996, 1997

x1
Intercontinental Cup: 1999

'THE BELFAST BOY'
GEORGE BEST

The incredible winger is one of United's all-time legends and a man many regard as our greatest ever player – here's why fans still sing his name at matches today...

You might have heard United fans signing songs about George Best at Old Trafford, or seen the famous United Trinity statue outside the stadium, and wondered just how good Bestie must have been. Well, he really was one of the greatest players that ever kicked a ball, and that's no exaggeration. He had skills like Lionel Messi and that's despite playing with heavy, old-fashioned footballs on horrible muddy pitches. He used to get kicked up and down the wing by angry defenders who couldn't deal with his skills, but he would just get up and beat them again!

His bravery and creativity made him an unbelievable player, he could score all different types of goals and he's rightly considered one

George came from Belfast in Northern Ireland — and one of the city's airports is named after him!

The Brazilian legend Pele once described Best as the greatest footballer in the world.

United's no.7 shirt is known the world over — but it was Best who made it famous!

'Bestie' once scored an incredible SIX goals in a game — against Northampton Town in a Cup tie in 1970.

GEORGE BEST

Wembley wonder! Best helps make United kings of Europe in 1968; (opposite, top) George was just a kid when he made the first team in '63, but was named the world's greatest five years later (opposite, bottom).

of United's all-time legends. His United story began when he was discovered playing football in Belfast, Northern Ireland, at the age of 15 and was brought over to play for the Reds' youth team.

He signed as a professional on his 17th birthday and was given his first-team debut by manager Sir Matt Busby a few months later in September 1963 against West Brom, and before long the United fans had fallen in love with this special player. He established himself as one of the most exciting players in England over the next couple of years, but the world stood up and took notice one night in March 1966 when, at the age of just 19, he starred in an incredible 5-1 win against Benfica in Portugal in the European Cup quarter-final, scoring twice. Benfica were one of the best teams in Europe, but Best was too good for them and it made him a massive star overnight. Despite the fame

GEORGE BEST

FRED'S FACTS!

470
Best played this many times for United, with 232 of these games coming at Old Trafford.

179
His overall goal total for the Reds, with only four players finding the net more often in our history.

37
That's how many caps George won for Northern Ireland, and he also scored nine goals for his country.

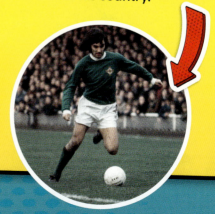

that followed, it was on the pitch when he was most at home, and after winning the league in 1967, Best and United were finally ready to conquer Europe.

After beating Real Madrid in the European Cup semi-finals, it was time to face our old rivals Benfica in the final of Europe's biggest club competition at Wembley. The final was incredibly close, with the scores level at 1-1 after 90 minutes. But just three minutes into

GEORGE BEST

extra-time, Best changed the game. Picking up the ball in the Benfica half, he dribbled around the Portuguese defence, took the ball round their keeper and rolled it into the empty net. Yes! United went on to score two more goals and we were crowned the first English team ever to become champions of Europe.

Later that year he was named the best player in Europe – all at the age of just 22! Sadly, this was to be the highlight of his career. As United struggled in the years after winning the European Cup, and after Busby retired from management, Best and United drifted apart, and he played his last game for the Reds on New Year's Day 1974. Despite this sad early departure, his legend status was guaranteed forever.

Simply the best.

x2
First Division:
1964/65,
1966/67

x2
Charity Shield:
1965 (shared),
1967 (shared)

x1
European Cup:
1968

x1
Ballon d'Or:
1968

GEORGE BEST

MAGIC MOMENT

Best's genius was already recognised in the UK and Ireland, but it was the night he blitzed Benfica in their own ground in March 1966 that saw him recognised by football fans in the rest of Europe and around the world. The next day he returned home wearing a sombrero, an image that has become one of the most famous United photos ever taken.

'THE GODFATHER'

SIR MATT BUSBY

The Scotsman arrived as an inexperienced coach but retired as one of the greatest ever, and is often described as the 'godfather of Manchester United'...

> As a kid, he'd often go down into the coal pits to help his dad, but he didn't want to do that as a job — he wanted to be a footballer!

> Sir Matt was manager of the Great Britain team at the 1948 olympics in London, reaching the semi-finals.

Sir Matt Busby was United manager from 1945 to 1969, briefly returning in 1970/71, and turned the club from a sleeping giant into one of the biggest names in world football. Across his 25 years in charge he built three great teams, survived a plane crash in which many of his players and staff were killed, and laid down the foundations for the club we see today. Few people, perhaps only Sir Alex Ferguson, have made a bigger impact on Manchester United Football Club.

When Matt was born, in a mining village in Scotland, the doctor told his mother that "a footballer has come into this house today". And he was right. Busby showed his talents

> Busby was offered the Real Madrid manager's job in 1956, but turned it down saying: "Manchester is my heaven."

> Only Sir Alex Ferguson (1,500 games) took charge of more United matches than Sir Matt.

SIR MATT BUSBY

Busby's 1948 FA Cup winners were his first great side, also winning the First Division title (now the Premier League) in 1952.

as a young player for a junior side in Stirlingshire called Denny Hibs and he was so good that he was signed up by Manchester City – yes, really! Over the next decade, Busby was one of the best players in the English leagues. He won the 1934 FA Cup with City and then moved to Liverpool – yes, he played for them too! – where he was made club captain.

Then came the Second World War, which interrupted Busby's playing career. He was a guest player for a few teams during the war, but towards the end of the conflict, United's chief scout Louis Rocca wrote him a letter referring to a mysterious 'job'. Rocca didn't want Liverpool – who Busby still played for – to know what was happening because the job was important. It was to become the next Manchester United manager as soon as the war was over.

In 1945, Busby accepted the offer and together with a small but fiery Welshman called Jimmy Murphy – his new assistant – the Scot revolutionised United and English football. The Reds played an attacking, entertaining style that cheered people up after the war and they won the FA Cup in 1948 and the league title in 1952 – United's first trophies for more than 30 years.

SIR MATT BUSBY

FRED'S FACTS!

1,140
Until Sir Alex Ferguson came along, this total of matches was the highest for any United boss.

576
This is how many wins Busby recorded as United manager – almost double the number of games he lost!

2,320
And this is how many goals his United side scored in all competitions. Wow!

While building that first great team, Busby and Murphy were also working hard behind the scenes, busy making sure replacements for their ageing players were lined up. They created a structure to find, sign and train the very best young players in Britain and Ireland. And soon, the 'Busby Babes' were born, nicknamed because Matt brought them into the first team at an unusually young age.

These 'Babes' included the big but skilful Duncan Edwards, wingers Eddie Colman and David Pegg, and a young lad from the north-east called Bobby Charlton. Busby managed his crop of young players perfectly and United won the league title in 1956 and 1957. The team's average age was only 21 – quite different to the average age of 26 for most title-winning teams.

Busby showed bravery in everything he did. Not only did he trust these 'Babes', but he also made sure United were the first English side to compete in the

SIR MATT BUSBY

European Cup, which later became the Champions League. In our first season, we lost to Real Madrid in the semi-finals but that just made Busby more determined to beat them the next year. Sadly, that chance would never come.

On 6 February 1958, while returning from a game against Red Star Belgrade, their plane crashed in Munich after a refuelling stop. A total of 23 people died, including eight players. Busby was badly injured. He was in hospital in Germany for nine weeks and on two occasions doctors and family prepared themselves for the worst. However, he slowly recovered and after initially considering leaving football – heartbroken by the loss of so many friends – he was convinced to continue and honour those who had died.

It took time, but Busby slowly created his third great side. Building around

Munich survivors Bill Foulkes and Charlton, more youngsters emerged from the youth system, while new signings like striker Denis Law came in.

United's lethal new goalscorer helped the Reds win the FA Cup in 1963, then league titles in 1965 and 1967. But it

TROPHY HAUL

x5 First Division: 1951/52, 1955/56, 1956/57, 1964/65, 1966/67

x1 European Cup: 1968

x2 FA Cup: 1948, 1963

x5 Charity Shield: 1952, 1956, 1957, 1965 (shared), 1967 (shared)

SIR MATT BUSBY

MAGIC MOMENT

Winning the European Cup in May 1968 – beating Benfica 4-1 at Wembley – was the undoubted peak of his managerial career, having first taken United into the competition in 1956/57. His pursuit of the trophy had almost cost him his life in Munich and he felt he had to honour the memories of the team he lost in the crash by winning the trophy. A dream realised.

was the European Cup that Busby and his players most wanted.

Ten years on from the tragedy, with a thrilling side led by the United Trinity of Charlton, Law and George Best, Busby finally achieved his dream: winning the European Cup. At the final whistle at Wembley, with United beating Benfica 4-1, the players ran straight over to Busby, because they knew what it meant to him. United became the first English side to conquer Europe, a proud achievement for which he was knighted, becoming Sir Matt Busby in July 1968.

Matt retired a season later, returned briefly as interim manager, and he then served as a club director for many years. He died in 1994 and is remembered as one of the greatest ever football managers.

'THE MAVERICK'
ERIC CANTONA

The French 'King' wore the sacred no.7 shirt with great distinction across five seasons with the Reds, etching his name into club legend with his remarkable talents...

After retiring from football, Eric became an actor and artist, and he also embarked on a musical career.

There are players in United's history with far more appearances and goals than Eric Cantona, but few can claim to have had more importance in the Reds' story than the fiery Frenchman.

Signed from fierce rivals Leeds United for just over £1 million in November 1992, Cantona turned out to be one of the greatest transfer bargains ever! When he arrived at Old Trafford, few could have imagined how well the move would have worked out. Eric had arrived in English football in January 1992, joining Leeds despite having already built himself a reputation as a troublemaker.

His list of controversies included a string of wild challenges, red cards and, in one case, throwing a ball at a referee! After he was

Eric featured in a music video for indie star Liam Gallagher — a renowned Manchester City supporter!

Eric became a successful player-manager with the French beach soccer team which won the European league and FIFA World Cup!

Cantona was famous for his brilliance from the penalty spot, sending the keeper the wrong way 17 times from the 18 he scored for United.

ERIC CANTONA

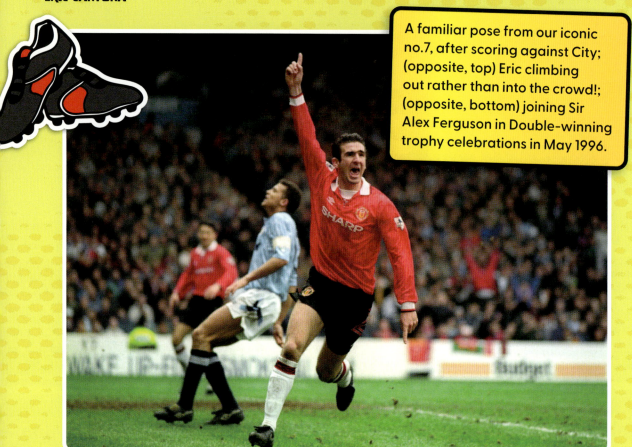

A familiar pose from our iconic no.7, after scoring against City; (opposite, top) Eric climbing out rather than into the crowd!; (opposite, bottom) joining Sir Alex Ferguson in Double-winning trophy celebrations in May 1996.

handed a one-month ban for that final act, he went to every member of the disciplinary panel and called each one an idiot. To call Cantona a colourful character would be an understatement!

Nevertheless, his talent was obvious. A powerful, skilful attacking threat, he had so much to offer any team. So, when Alex Ferguson was looking for a striker, French legend Michel Platini advised him to move for Cantona, saying: "You should sign him. His character is underestimated – he just needs a bit of understanding."

Eric is often referred to as the last part of Ferguson's first great United team. At the time of Cantona's arrival, the Reds had gone over 26 years without winning a league title. Although there had been some success, including three trophies in the previous three years, that long wait to be English champions had been eating away at everybody inside Old Trafford – especially after being on course to win the league in 1991/92, only to then lose it in the final few games. "For me, Eric was the last piece in the jigsaw of what

ERIC CANTONA

FRED'S FACTS!

185
The Frenchman played this many times for the Reds, and his importance to the team was always huge.

82
This is how many goals Eric scored for United, with his best season being 1993/94: 25 goals from 49 matches.

45
Number of international caps won with France between 1987 and 1995 – he also scored 20 goals!

the gaffer was trying to achieve," said legendary United captain Bryan Robson. "We knew the quality that he was bringing into the squad. Everybody had a lot to say about his character and his charisma before he arrived at United, but that was never going to be a problem for the group of lads at our club."

Cantona not only had an immediate impact on the Reds' performances during games, he also inspired his team-mates to train better, leading to a huge improvement throughout the squad.

ERIC CANTONA

MAGIC MOMENT

After returning from suspension to inspire his side to regain the Premier League title in 1995/96, Eric went a step further by securing the Reds' second Double in style: volleying home a brilliant late winner at Wembley to beat Liverpool in the FA Cup final!

Within six months, the long wait was over and United were league champions for the first time since 1966/67! Not that Ferguson's side were finished there: further titles followed in 1993/94, 1995/96 and 1996/97 – plus two FA Cups – ensuring the Reds were champions in four of Cantona's five seasons as a Red. The only exception in that sequence came in 1994/95, when Eric was absent from January onwards due to a long-term ban from the Football Association for scuffling with a Crystal Palace supporter. When he was later asked for his career highlights, Cantona said this was one of his favourite moments, as he felt he had responded justifiably to being abused by the fan.

ERIC CANTONA

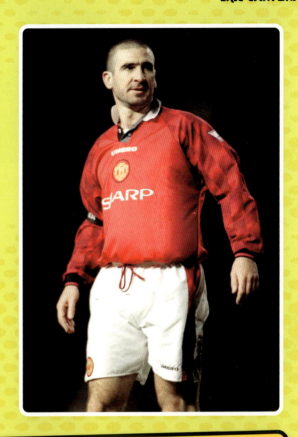

For most, however, his highlights involve his brilliance on the ball, such as a sensational touch-and-volley in an FA Cup win at Wimbledon, a wonderful assist for Denis Irwin against Spurs, or his ferocious free-kick against Arsenal.

However, most famous of all was his 1996 goal against Sunderland, where he spun away from three players, played a one-two, then chipped in a jaw-dropping finish via the inside of the post. Old Trafford has seen some truly great goals, but few were scored – and celebrated (right) – with as much swagger as Cantona's iconic effort.

Surprisingly, it would prove to be one of his final acts as a Red, as he stunned football by retiring aged 30 in May 1997. Yet, even though fans would have loved to enjoy him for longer, Cantona's legacy had already long been set in stone.

TROPHY HAUL

x4
Premier League:
1992/93, 1993/94, 1995/96, 1996/97

x2
FA Cup:
1994, 1996

x3
Charity Shield:
1993, 1994, 1996

'CARRAS'
MICHAEL CARRICK

Here's the story of a multiple trophy-winner and one of United's most dependable midfielders — one who always played with a cool head...

Throughout his 12 years as a Red, holding midfielder Michael Carrick kept United's engine ticking over with a simplicity of play that proved so vital to the team's success. It wasn't that he was without a flourish in his play, rather that his dedication to the team and calm presence in the middle of the pitch allowed his more creative team-mates to express themselves. He was vital to the success enjoyed by Sir Alex Ferguson's side from 2007 to 2013, a period in which he became one of the most decorated English footballers ever.

Michael was born on 28 July 1981 in Wallsend, Tyneside. He was a boyhood Newcastle United fan and played for his local side Wallsend Boys Club, who famously produced ex-Reds captain

Carrick was still at West Ham when he made his debut for England, aged 19, against Mexico in a friendly in 2001.

Michael's nickname at United was 'Carras', a shortened version of his surname.

Michael picked up a winner's medal in all seven competitions he played in with United. Nice!

Carrick was very popular in the United dressing room, being voted Players' Player of the Year in 2012/13.

MICHAEL CARRICK

Carrick's silverware haul while at United was an incredible 18 trophies, including five Premier League titles – the last of which was won in May 2013 (above) – and the much-cherished Champions League crown, proudly claimed in 2008 (right).

Steve Bruce, and England internationals Peter Beardsley and Alan Shearer, to name just a few. Carrick was signed up by West Ham aged 16, and two years later he won the 1999 FA Youth Cup with the Hammers' Under-18s. Loan spells with Swindon Town and Birmingham City followed, then he established himself in the heart of the West Ham senior side. In 2004, Carrick switched across London to play for Tottenham Hotspur, where he impressed so much that in summer 2006, Sir Alex Ferguson signed him for United, giving him Roy Keane's no.16 shirt. No pressure then, Michael!

In his first season (2006/07), Carrick struck up an instinctive partnership with Paul Scholes in the centre of midfield as the Reds looked to win the Premier League for the first time in four years.

They combined beautifully: the new man sweeping up and keeping things running smoothly with a wide range of passes, while Scholes was always probing and looking to burst forward to score. They were key to toppling Chelsea as English champions, as United thrilled crowds with a stunning brand of attacking football led by Wayne Rooney and Cristiano Ronaldo. A Champions

MICHAEL CARRICK

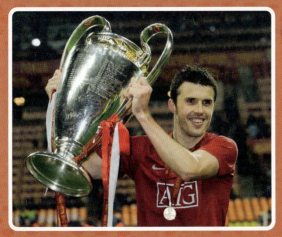

FRED'S FACTS!

League semi-final defeat to AC Milan ended our European hopes, but only after an amazing 7-1 quarter-final win against Roma in which Carrick scored two stunning goals. Look them up on YouTube!

The following season, 2007/08, the side grew in strength again and this time realised their European dream. With the Premier League crown retained on the final day against Wigan Athletic, United met their main title rivals Chelsea in the Champions League final. After a 1-1 draw across 120 minutes, the game was settled by penalties – United winning 6-5, with Carrick converting his spot-kick. He was a European champion; then a world champion some six months later when he helped the Reds to defeat LDU Quito 1-0 in the FIFA Club World Cup in Japan.

Further success followed for Michael: Premier League titles in 2009 (to make it three in a row), 2011 and 2013, the FA Cup in 2016, the League Cup in 2009, 2010 and 2017, the Europa League in 2017, plus six Community Shields.

464
Think of how many kilometres Michael would have covered in playing this many matches!

24
He wasn't a prolific scorer for the Reds but his game was about so much more than finding the net.

34
He represented England this many times across his career, with 27 of his caps coming as a United player.

MICHAEL CARRICK

MAGIC MOMENT

Carrick's first away goal for United was a massively important one. His 86th-minute left-footed strike at Wigan Athletic, in May 2009, gave the Reds a 2-1 win and meant only a point was needed from the final two games to secure league title no.18 for the Reds.

While international recognition was only occasional (he won 34 England caps), he was certainly appreciated by United fans and team-mates.

"Carrick's like a piano," Gary Neville once said of him. "When you play with him you think there is authority, control, peace. Sometimes you don't want people running around like flies. Scholes and Carrick together was peaceful. It was like going into a bar and hearing a piano playing. Relaxing!"

His partner Scholes was also glowing in praise, saying: "I remember Michael coming in and taking over the no.16 shirt from Roy Keane, one of the Premier

MICHAEL CARRICK

League's best ever midfielders. He had big boots to fill, but I think he proved that he was more than worthy of the shirt. I loved playing with him."

Carrick retired at the end of 2017/18, having played 464 games for the Reds, scoring 24 goals. He became a coach at United, leaving in 2021, before being named Middlesbrough boss. He's since shown the same cool-headed approach in coaching as he displayed across a decade of controlling United's midfield.

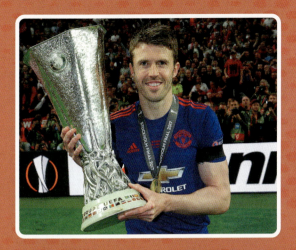

x5

Premier League:
2006/07, 2007/08,
2008/09, 2010/11, 2012/13

x1

Champions League:
2008

x1

FA Cup:
2016

x3

League Cup:
2009, 2010,
2017

x6

Community Shield:
2007, 2008, 2010,
2011, 2013, 2016

x1

Europa League:
2017

x1

Club World Cup:
2008

'THE GENTLEMAN OF FOOTBALL'

SIR BOBBY CHARLTON

One third of the 'United Trinity', winner of the *Ballon d'Or*, a world champion with the Three Lions and one of the most famous players ever to pull on the red shirt…

If you had to pick one man to represent Manchester United, there really is no debate. Sir Bobby Charlton was a midfielder who could score with either foot from outside the box, dribble past opponents like a Brazilian, and assist team-mates with the very best passes. But he was also so much more. He was a gentleman – a quiet, modest man who simply loved to play, watch and teach football. And while he wasn't loud on or off the pitch, he had an inner fire that everyone admired, because his career and life became a tribute to the friends he lost along the way.

Charlton became a hero to millions, not just in Manchester, or the United Kingdom, and not just to United fans, but to fans of football all around the world. In fact, it is fair to say

Charlton is the only United player to win the World Cup, European Cup and Ballon d'Or while with the club.

Sir Bobby was a very clean footballer – during his 864 games for United and England he was never sent off!

In case he didn't make the grade as a professional footballer, for a while as a United trainee he was also doing an apprenticeship as an electrical engineer!

The South Stand at old Trafford was renamed the 'Sir Bobby Charlton Stand' in his honour in 2016.

SIR BOBBY CHARLTON

Charlton was one of the famous 'Busby Babes' and on his debut against Charlton Athletic (yep, honestly!) he scored twice to show United fans his potential. He quickly became a key figure for the Reds (right).

that for many years, the words 'Bobby Charlton' were two of the most widely used in the English language across the world. Imagine a player as famous as Cristiano Ronaldo or Lionel Messi, but who played when football was shown on black-and-white TVs! That was Sir Bobby.

Charlton was born in a mining town called Ashington, near Newcastle, into a family of football fanatics. Several members of his family played the professional game, with the most famous being his uncle Jackie Milburn, who played for Newcastle United. A number of clubs were interested in signing Bobby, but it was Manchester United that he chose. He had heard the team win the 1948 FA Cup final on the radio, seen newspaper articles about the exciting project led by Matt Busby, and knew that Old Trafford was the right place for him to fulfil his potential.

He moved to Manchester in 1953 and called it 'paradise' as he became friends with other talented youngsters like Duncan Edwards and Eddie Colman. They won the FA Youth Cup together – three times in Charlton's case – before becoming first-team players. Bobby's debut came on 6 October 1956, and it was the most magical of moments (see above). He had waited a long time for the chance

SIR BOBBY CHARLTON

FRED'S FACTS!

758
Only Ryan Giggs has played more times for United than Charlton, whose Reds career lasted from 1956-1973.

249
This is Charlton's incredible goal tally for the Reds, only beaten by the 253 scored by Wayne Rooney.

106
Bobby won this many caps for England, becoming the second player to reach a century after Billy Wright.

– longer than many of his friends in the youth team – but he made the most of it, scoring two fantastic goals on his debut, a very rare achievement. Amazingly, he did so with a sprained ankle – being so desperate to play that he hid the injury from the United coaches.

Charlton helped United to win the league title in 1957, but he was still fighting to become one of the first-choice players in the Reds' talented attack. He was still young and knew his time would come, and in February 1958, he scored twice as United drew with Red Star Belgrade in Yugoslavia (now Serbia), to claim a place in the semi-finals of the European Cup.

During United's return home, the team's plane crashed in Munich killing 23 people, including eight of Charlton's team-mates. Bobby survived with minor injuries, but his life would never be the same again. His

SIR BOBBY CHARLTON

MAGIC MOMENT

Here's Bobby on the greatest night of his United life in May 1968, running around Wembley Stadium with the European Cup and his jubilant team-mates. He scored two goals to help the Reds beat Benfica 4-1 that night, a fitting tribute to the team-mates he'd lost in Munich.

best friends were gone. He found it hard to talk about them and he put his energy into ensuring United would rise again.

He played a month after the crash and, incredibly, helped United – with only half a squad – reach the FA Cup final. They lost to Bolton Wanderers at Wembley, but Bobby, still only 20 years old, was now at the centre of the United rebuild.

Over the next decade, Charlton became one of the best players in the world and was joined at Old Trafford by the fantastic striker Denis Law and the clever winger George Best. Together, the 'United Trinity' won everything, as a team and individually. There is a statue of them outside Old Trafford. All three won the *Ballon d'Or*, Charlton doing so in 1966.

SIR BOBBY CHARLTON

Having won the FA Cup with Law in 1963 – beating Leicester City 3-1 – he was then a league title winner again in 1965 (alongside Law and Best). The Reds fell short in the quest for the European Cup in 1966, losing to Partizan Belgrade in the semi-finals. For Charlton, though, there was to be a happy ending to the season as he played a key role in helping England to win the World Cup. He was named in the team of the tournament and then voted the best player on the planet (right).

The following season he won a third league title and then, finally, the European Cup in May 1968. It was the ultimate tribute to his friends who died in the Munich Air Disaster 10 years earlier, and fitting that he should be captain on the night and lift the big-handled trophy.

When Charlton left five years later, he was seen as United's greatest-ever player. He returned to Old Trafford to become a director in 1984 and served in that role until his death in 2023. He could often be found in the dressing room after matches, encouraging the new generation of players, and was loved by everyone at United – a club that he loved with all his heart.

TROPHY HAUL

- **x3** First Division: 1956/57, 1964/65, 1966/67
- **x1** European Cup: 1968
- **x1** FA Cup: 1963
- **x2** Charity Shield: 1965 (shared), 1967 (shared)
- **x1** World Cup: 1966
- **x1** Ballon d'Or: 1966

'THE QUEEN OF STOPS'
MARY EARPS

A true trailblazer between the sticks, the Lioness is a Reds legend and a national treasure, having inspired so many young girls to pick up a pair of gloves…

It was a sad day when Mary Earps left the Reds in the summer of 2024, but taking on a new challenge – in this case moving to France to join *Premiere Ligue* giants PSG – is something the much-loved goalkeeper has done many times throughout her life. She departed United as a real hero, who'll always be given a warm welcome whenever she pays a visit to Leigh Sports Village or Old Trafford.

Memorably, Mary was named the world's best women's goalkeeper by FIFA in 2022 and 2023, as well as winning the BBC's prestigious Sports Personality of the Year award in 2023, but what made Mary's long path to the very top so inspiring is how she overcame many obstacles along the way before joining United in July 2019.

Before joining the Reds, Earps played for eight clubs – including VFL Wolfsburg in Germany – before settling at United in 2019.

Mary became United Women's fifth centurion in October 2023, joining Ella Toone, Katie Zelem, Millie Turner and Leah Galton in reaching 100 appearances for the club.

In 2022/23, Mary claimed the WSL Golden Glove award in record-breaking style, after keeping 14 clean sheets from 22 games.

Earps became the first female professional footballer to be honoured with a wax figure at Madame Tussauds in London in August 2024!

MARY EARPS

Mary always put her body on the line for the Reds, and despite being a fierce competitor she would often smile along the way (right)!

Like a lot of youngsters in sport, Mary had self-doubt at times, not believing she was quite good enough to make a proper career out of doing what she loved. If you're a goalkeeper reading this you might be able to relate to that – even the smallest of mistakes often leads to an opposition goal, so it's a position that requires real mental toughness!

Nottingham-born Mary was 26 years old before joining United, with her senior career until that point taking her from Leicester City, to Nottingham Forest, to Doncaster Rovers Belles, to Birmingham City, to Bristol City, to Reading, and then to Wolfsburg – her first foreign adventure!

While Earps didn't play too many games in Germany throughout that 2018/19 season, United manager Casey Stoney had already seen enough of Mary's ability and attitude between the sticks to persuade her to return to English football as mum-to-be Siobhan Chamberlain's replacement in the United goal.

And how Mary thrived in the famous shirt, quickly winning the hearts of fans

MARY EARPS

FRED'S FACTS!

125

After becoming the fifth player to reach 100 appearances for United Women, she'd take it up to this number in the 2024 FA Cup final.

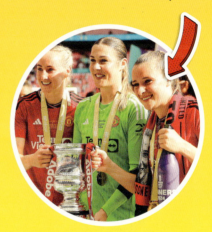

50

In addition to her century of games for the Reds, she's also excelled in goal for England and in 2024 reached the 50-cap milestone.

at United Women's LSV home with her courageous keeping and (very vocal!) leadership – goalkeepers need to be loud, and Mary definitely knows how to be!

Over the next five seasons she wouldn't miss a single minute of Women's Super League action for the Reds, racking up 125 appearances in all competitions, with so many commanding performances along the way – such as her brilliant home debut against Arsenal in September 2019 (when she was so unfortunate to be on the losing side) right up to April

MARY EARPS

2024, when she did as much as anyone in helping United finally beat Chelsea to progress to the Women's FA Cup final.

On the international stage, it would be England's Euros triumph in 2022 that really pushed Earps into the wider spotlight beyond those who'd already seen her shine in the WSL. With the Lionesses winning the tournament, Earps conceded just two goals in six games, making the Team of the Tournament and getting to revel in the Wembley celebrations alongside some of her United team-mates. *'Good times never seemed so good!'*

When not wearing the goalie gloves, Mary has always been one to challenge herself just as much away from the pitch. As a youngster she combined her goalkeeping with getting a degree – in information management and business studies at Loughborough University – and she continues to educate herself in that area. "I love learning how the business world works," says Mary, who also admits enjoying picking up new languages, first German, and since her move to Paris, French. Mary, you are *magnifique*!

So who knows what the future will bring for United's former no.27 (her preferred shirt number) when she finally hangs up her gloves, but she's such an inspiring figure, you can guarantee she won't wish for a quiet retirement. Speaking soon after leaving the Reds in 2024, Mary admitted: "I'm a very ambitious person, a very hard-working person, and to try and push boundaries and be a pioneer for change is something I really enjoy doing."

Talk about a trailblazer...

TROPHY HAUL

x1 Women's FA Cup: 2024

x1 European Championship: 2022

MARY EARPS

MAGIC MOMENT

Her gravity-defying leap against Chelsea in the 2023/24 Women's FA Cup semi-final, to deny former United team-mate Lauren James an equaliser. With Mary needing to shift direction before making the leap, her quick feet set her up for a famous stop. United would hang on for the win, before lifting the trophy the following month (left), with that save proving to be one of the defining moments of the glorious Cup run.

'THE POWERHOUSE'
DUNCAN EDWARDS

This extraordinary midfielder was one of the star names of the great Busby Babes – a humble player who seemed to have the ability to do everything on a football pitch...

When your grandparents and parents tell you about the finest United players from the past, they probably mention people like George Best, Roy Keane, Cristiano Ronaldo and Wayne Rooney. There's also a good chance they've mentioned the name Duncan Edwards, too.

Who was he? 'Big Duncan', as his team-mates and fans would call him, was a truly brilliant footballer, and an important part of the great 'Busby Babes' team of the 1950s (so called because the players were so young). Many believe he could have become one of the world's greatest ever footballers – and plenty of fans who watched him say he already was! Sadly, Duncan died of injuries suffered in the

Duncan's United debut came against Cardiff City on 4 April 1953, but United lost the game 1-4. Thankfully much better was to come!

As well as his five goals for England, he scored five goals in six appearances for England Under-23s.

Edwards played against Manchester City more than any other team for United (11 matches).

Duncan was named the third best player in the world in 1957, finishing behind Ballon d'Or winner Alfredo Di Stefano and England team-mate Billy Wright.

DUNCAN EDWARDS

Duncan was a midfield powerhouse for the Babes, an enforcer with sublime skills, who was a real hero to youngsters of the 1950s (right).

Munich Air Disaster of 6 February 1958, when 23 people were killed in a plane crash as Matt Busby's team, staff and journalists returned from a European Cup match against Red Star Belgrade in modern-day Serbia. Eight of those were players, with Duncan tragically losing his life in hospital 15 days after the crash.

While there is always sadness when talking about the brilliant midfielder, who was good enough to also play in defence or attack, there is also joy in discussing his wonderful displays for club and country.

He was only 21 when he died but he'd been dominating games for years with his hard tackling like Keane, excellent ball control like Paul Scholes, and driving runs like Bryan Robson.

All of England's top clubs had wanted to sign Duncan on his 16th birthday, the age a player had to be to join a professional club. Although he was born and bred in Dudley, in the West Midlands, and was wanted by his local teams Wolves and Aston Villa, there was only one club he wanted to play for... Manchester United! It proved the right choice, as he helped the Reds' brilliant youth team win the FA Youth Cup in 1953, 1954 and 1955.

It is said that Duncan was built like a man while still only a boy, and it was while inspiring the youth team that he

DUNCAN EDWARDS

FRED'S FACTS!

177
Duncan played this many times for United prior to his tragic death in Munich, aged just 21.

21
He was so good he could play anywhere on the pitch, making this goal tally an impressive one.

18
Duncan won this many England caps, scoring five goals – he surely would have gone to be a World Cup winner in 1966.

also began impressing for the senior team. He made his debut for United aged 16, and then for England aged 18 – being the then-youngest player to represent the Three Lions since before the Second World War. From October 1953 he became a regular for Matt Busby's side, going on to win the league title in both 1956 and 1957.

Big Duncan's favoured position was 'left-half', which in today's game would be a deep-lying midfield role. His strength and power were always impressive, he could pass equally well with either foot, with his shooting from distance becoming legendary. He scored 21 times for United and five times for England.

The great Sir Bobby Charlton, who is seen as one of football's finest ever players, famously said of Duncan: "He

DUNCAN EDWARDS

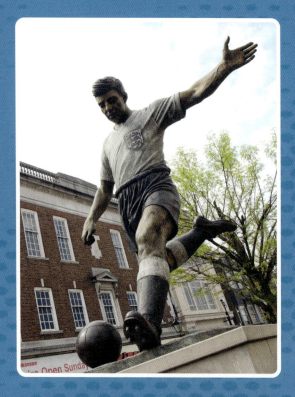

was the greatest player I ever played with, without any question. He was unstoppable, literally unstoppable. I've never known anyone so gifted, so strong and with such a presence."

Edwards died way too young, having played 177 times for United and 18 times for England. How good he could have become we can only guess, but many experts believe he was destined to be captain of the Reds and Three Lions for many years to come.

Today, there's a statue of Duncan in the centre of his hometown of Dudley (left), two stained glass windows in a nearby church, and his grave is visited regularly by Manchester United fans. His life may have been cruelly cut short, but he'll always remain a true Reds legend.

TROPHY HAUL

x2 First Division: 1955/56, 1956/57

x2 Charity Shield: 1956, 1957

DUNCAN EDWARDS

MAGIC MOMENT

Duncan was United's star man when the best club side in the world, Real Madrid, visited Old Trafford for the stadium's first-ever European tie in April 1957. Trailing 1-3 from the first leg, and 2-0 down back in Manchester, Big Dunc upped his game and led the fightback. His determination helped to pull the score back to 2-2 on the night, launching an unbeaten home run in European games that would last for 40 years.

'THE STYLISH CENTRE-BACK'

RIO FERDINAND

One of the most successful defenders in our history, the multiple trophy-winner was a smooth operator in defence for well over a decade under Sir Alex Ferguson...

These days Rio Ferdinand is one of the most recognisable faces among all the football pundits on TV, but when you look at what he achieved in his incredible playing career, you'll see he's very, very well qualified to talk about the game! There are few defenders in English football history who won as much as he did, with the FA Cup the only big trophy he didn't manage to lift (although he did come very close!).

Rio was born in Peckham, south-east London, and started his professional career at West Ham, making his debut for the Hammers at the age of 17. Everyone in football was talking about this talented young defender, and United even made a cheeky bid to sign the teenager, but West Ham were having none of it!

Rio was named in the PFA's Premier League Team of the Year — voted for by fellow top-flight professionals — five times while a United player.

Rio's little brother Anton was also a professional footballer, playing for West Ham, Sunderland and QPR among other teams in a long career.

The defender had a reputation among his team-mates for being a prankster, and even made a TV show called Rio's World Cup Wind-Ups!

When he was a kid, Rio went to the Central School of Ballet in London for four years, before deciding to concentrate on football.

RIO FERDINAND

Rio was captain when the Reds were crowned FIFA Club World champions in Japan in December 2008, and (right) he was always a match for any centre-forward!

He became a fan favourite with the London club and was named Hammer of the Year in 1998, but it wasn't long before his first big move came, and it was to Leeds United.

Believe it or not, Leeds were a much more successful club than West Ham at that point, and it took a British transfer record to seal the deal. He spent two years in Yorkshire, becoming the club captain and leading them to the Champions League semi-finals. But then having played for two Uniteds – West Ham and Leeds – the big one came calling... Manchester United!

He signed for the Reds in the summer of 2002, which was a hugely controversial move because there's a long-running rivalry between Leeds and United. To say the locals in Yorkshire weren't happy was an understatement! The last big player to move between the two clubs was Eric Cantona, and that transfer didn't turn out too bad! Again the move made Rio the world's most expensive defender, and pretty soon he was to prove that he was

RIO FERDINAND

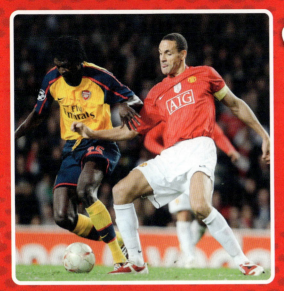

FRED'S FACTS!

455
Rio's appearance total is in the top 20 all-time list for the club, with only six defenders racking up more games.

8
He didn't score that often, but when he did they were usually spectacular, like his two goals against Liverpool.

81
Ferdinand won this many caps for England, scoring three goals and captaining his country seven times.

worth every penny. He became United's new no.5 and in his first season he won the first of six league winner's medals.

He had a number of centre-back partners that season, but it would be a few years before the arrival of a player who made the Reds one of the hardest teams to score against for a few years... Nemanja Vidic! Together Rio and Vida became one of United's greatest ever centre-back partnerships, and with Edwin van der Sar behind them in goal, it set up United to have one of the most successful periods in the club's history.

Rio's reputation as one of the world's greatest defenders was well-earned, but it's fair to say he was less well-known for scoring at the other end of the pitch. It took until his fourth season at United before he scored his first goal for the Reds, in a 4-0 win over Wigan at Old Trafford in the Premier League, but he followed it up

RIO FERDINAND

MAGIC MOMENT

Rio's job was stopping goals but arguably his outstanding moment as a Red came as the match-winning goalscorer against our main rivals Liverpool. That was in January 2006 at Old Trafford, with Rio leaping highest to head in a 90th-minute winner from a corner at the Stretford End. The stuff of dreams for every United supporter!

with another one just a few weeks later against West Brom, and then saved the best for the next month when he scored the winning goal in the last minute against our biggest rivals Liverpool (above), in front of the Stretford End. Get in!

An even rarer event happened in an FA Cup quarter-final against Portsmouth in 2008... he went in goal! Keeper Edwin van der Sar had to go off injured, and then when sub stopper Tomasz Kuszczak was sent off having conceded a penalty, Rio volunteered to put on the gloves and the goalie's jersey. Sadly Portsmouth scored the penalty that was to follow, but at least Rio dived the right way...

There's no doubt that Rio's most successful year was in 2008, when he

RIO FERDINAND

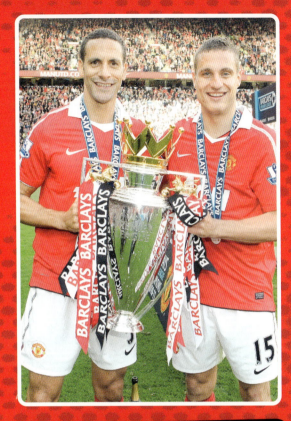

was a huge player in the United team that won the Premier League, the Champions League and, finally, the Club World Cup. He captained the Reds in United's famous UCL final victory over Chelsea and lifted the trophy along with Ryan Giggs on that rainy night in Moscow. It was a career highlight, and he saved another one for Sir Alex Ferguson's last ever game at Old Trafford as United manager, when he scored the winning goal in that emotional match against Swansea City. By that point Rio's time at United was drawing to a close, and he completed one more season for the Reds before moving to QPR where he was reunited with his first-ever manager, Harry Redknapp. Rio hung up his boots at the end of the 2014/15 season, but is often back at Old Trafford cheering on United as part of his media duties.

Once a Red, always a Red.

x6
Premier League:
2002/03, 2006/07,
2007/08, 2008/09,
2010/11, 2012/13

x1
Champions League:
2008

x2
League Cup:
2006, 2009

x4
Community Shield:
2003, 2007, 2008, 2011

x1
Club World Cup:
2008

'THE BOSS'

SIR ALEX FERGUSON

A man who embraced United traditions, yet reinvented the club and powered us to dizzying new heights. The greatest football manager ever? Quite possibly...

Many people consider Sir Alex Ferguson to be the greatest Manchester United manager in history. And is it any wonder? He won 13 Premier League titles with the Reds! But the number of trophies he lifted only tells half the story, really. The main reason for his legend is that he returned the club to our rightful place at the pinnacle of English and European football, after decades in the wilderness. And then he kept us there for 20 years!

It all started for Sir Alex in Govan, Scotland, where he was good enough to play professionally for the team he supported, Rangers. But Ferguson really made his name after hanging up his boots, as the manager

Sir Alex Ferguson also managed Scotland at the 1986 World Cup, following the death of his great friend Jock Stein.

Ferguson said that he worked with four world-class players at United: Eric Cantona, Ryan Giggs, Paul Scholes and Cristiano Ronaldo.

He won the Premier League Manager of the Month award 27 times!

As a young striker for Dunfermline, Ferguson was the Scottish league's top scorer in 1965/66.

SIR ALEX FERGUSON

of Aberdeen. The Dons had won the Scottish league just once in their entire history when Ferguson arrived. But against overwhelming odds, they did so three times in six seasons under his leadership. Even more remarkably, they beat Real Madrid in the 1983 European Cup Winners' Cup final. To put those achievements in perspective, nobody has beaten Real Madrid in a major European final since! Aberdeen also remain the last Scottish club other than the 'Old Firm' (Rangers or Celtic) to win the league.

So when manager Ron Atkinson left United in 1986, Sir Alex was the club's clear choice to replace him. But what a challenge for the Scot! United had not won the English league title for 19 years, and our arch-rivals, Liverpool, were shovelling up titles and European Cups for fun. It was slow-going for the first few seasons: United finished as low as 11th and 13th. But the club kept believing in Ferguson and in 1990, were rewarded with his first trophy: the FA Cup. The following year, we added the Cup Winners' Cup with a memorable 2-1 victory over Johan Cruyff's Barcelona 'Dream Team' in Rotterdam. Then, buoyed by the emergence of generational talent Ryan Giggs and the addition of maverick French genius Eric Cantona, United finally became champions again in 1992/93 – the first season of the Premier League era.

Once Sir Alex had taken the Reds to the top, his incredible management skills became even more obvious.

In a career covering 1,500 games as Reds boss, Sir Alex collected a whopping 38 trophies, including three domestic Doubles (above), the last of which was upgraded to a Treble in 1999 after he oversaw our remarkable last-gasp Champions League win over Bayern Munich in the Nou Camp.

He was able to motivate players to keep on winning titles: a first 'Double' came in 1994. He also showed a knack for regenerating his team: after selling key players Mark Hughes, Paul Ince and Andrei Kanchelskis in the summer of 1995, he embedded several youth players like David Beckham, Gary Neville and Paul Scholes into the side, winning the Double again in 1996. Four more Premier League titles were hoovered up in the next five years and, in 1998/99, United became the

SIR ALEX FERGUSON

first English club to win the Treble, after snatching the Champions League from Bayern Munich thanks to two injury-time goals from Teddy Sheringham and Ole Gunnar Solskjaer. The United boss was knighted later that year!

After an eighth Premier League title in 2002/03, United took something of a dip. Long-term captain Roy Keane departed in 2005, and Arsene Wenger's Arsenal and Jose Mourinho's Chelsea overtook the Reds. Some questioned whether Sir Alex had passed his peak. But the wily Scot was simply cooking up his next great team, built around the phenomenal twin talents of Cristiano Ronaldo and Wayne Rooney (below). In 2006/07, supported by the now experienced Giggs, Neville and Scholes, plus the steely defensive harmony of Rio Ferdinand and Nemanja Vidic, the pair blasted United

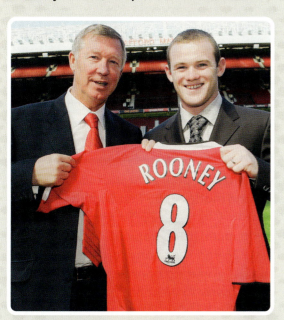

FRED'S FACTS!

1,500
No manager has been in charge for more United matches than Sir Alex.

895
This is how many wins the Reds enjoyed under Ferguson, with 338 draws and 267 defeats.

2,769
What a goal count this is from his time as boss (not to mention a goal difference of +1,404!) – Sir Alex's approach was always to attack, attack, attack!

SIR ALEX FERGUSON

MAGIC MOMENT

It should be hard to pick just one moment from his 27 years as United boss, but you can't really look beyond the Champions League final in May 1999. Trailing 0-1 to Bayern Munich, Ferguson put on two substitutes to try to turn things around. And didn't they just! Sheringham and Solskjaer scored the two injury-time goals to clinch the Treble, in one of sport's most thrilling climaxes.

to the first of three consecutive titles. In 2008, Ferguson also won the Champions League again, via a dramatic penalty shoot-out over domestic rivals Chelsea in Moscow. Ronaldo was sold to Real Madrid in 2009, but Ferguson managed to win two further championships. The first, in 2011, took United to 19 titles, one beyond Liverpool's historic tally. The second made us the first English club in history to reach 20. Sir Alex finally announced his retirement in May 2013, after 26 years in charge and 38 trophies. His last game – a bonkers 5-5 league draw away to West Bromwich Albion – was his 1,500th. What an icon!

SIR ALEX FERGUSON

TROPHY HAUL

x13

Premier League:
1992/93, 1993/94, 1995/96, 1996/97, 1998/99, 1999/2000, 2000/01, 2002/03, 2006/07, 2007/08, 2008/09, 2010/11, 2012/13

x5

FA Cup:
1990, 1994, 1996, 1999, 2004

x4

League Cup:
1992, 2006, 2009, 2010

x2

Champions League:
1999, 2008

x1

European Cup Winners' Cup
1991

x10

Charity/Community Shield:
1990 (shared), 1993, 1994, 1996, 1997, 2003, 2007, 2008, 2010, 2011

x1

Club World Cup:
2008

x1

European Super Cup:
1991

x1

Intercontinental Cup:
1999

67

BRUNO FERNANDES

'OUR PORTUGUESE MAGNIFICO'

BRUNO FERNANDES

Looking at the career so far of one of United's most creative recent players – a gifted midfielder who chased his dream of becoming a Red…

Bruno likes to celebrate a goal by covering his ears with his hands – it's a tribute to his daughter, who when young would often do the same when Dad asked her to put her toys away!

He really had a soft spot for United as a kid and said he had 'tears in his eyes' when he signed for the Reds in 2020.

When you get a footballer who can perform magic tricks with his feet and runs for 90 minutes without stopping, every single week, he becomes truly loved by fans. And Bruno Fernandes is loved at Manchester United.

Bruno's career is a tale of hard work. As a boy, he dreamed of playing in the Premier League and playing for United, but it took years. He came from a family of good football players and played on the streets with his older brother. He followed a Portuguese team called Boavista, going to games both home and away, but he also loved watching United.

Bruno was nine years old when Cristiano Ronaldo joined the Reds. He dreamed of doing what Ronaldo was doing: scoring goals

Fernandes had been named United's Player of the Year on three occasions up to summer 2024. Only Cristiano Ronaldo and David De Gea have won more (four wins each).

Bruno was a centre-back when he was younger, and only changed to attacking midfield when he was 15!

BRUNO FERNANDES

Bruno was made captain (right) ahead of the 2023/24 season, but was already a leader on the pitch for the Reds – whether scoring, creating for others or driving the team on.

for United and Portugal, and winning trophies. And eventually, he did. But his journey was very different. Ronaldo signed for United aged 17. At the same age, Bruno also took the brave decision to move to another country. Except, he went to Italy – where he played for a team in their second league (*Serie B*) called Novara.

He didn't speak Italian when he moved, but he soon learned. He labelled things in his room with the Italian words – like *'sedia'* on a chair, or *'tavolo'* on a table – to help him. On the pitch, his performances were so good that the biggest Italian clubs wanted to sign Bruno and he had time at Udinese and Sampdoria before returning to Portugal to sign for Sporting Club, in Lisbon. He was named the league's best player for two years in a row and in one season scored 33 goals! No midfielder in European football has scored more goals in a single year.

In January 2020, Bruno finally got his dream. He signed for United. Fans immediately saw a player who worked as hard as anyone else and had the skill to

BRUNO FERNANDES

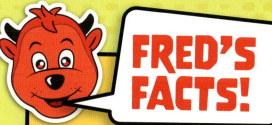

FRED'S FACTS!

233
Bruno's appearance total ahead of the 2024/25 season, with him rarely missing a match for the Reds.

79
His goal return is also healthy, with Bruno averaging a goal about every three games from midfield.

64
Fernandes is a regular for Portugal, and this was his appearance total at the end of 2023/24 (scoring 22 goals).

beat every opponent. He only had a few months to show his ability that season, but he was so good – scoring 12 goals in 22 games – that he was voted United's best player of the campaign.

He won the same award the next year, when games were played without fans in stadiums due to Covid-19. In that period, Fernandes was at the centre of everything good for United. In one game at West Ham, he came off the bench at half-time to create an amazing eight chances. The Reds were 1-0 down when he came on, then scored three goals in 13 minutes to win. But special moments like these were without fans inside the ground, and Bruno longed for them to return so he could celebrate with them.

Over the next few years, Bruno continued to do the incredible, or whatever was needed, for United to win.

BRUNO FERNANDES

In one season, he created more chances than any other United player had done for 20 years. The Reds won the League Cup in 2023 and Bruno was captain for the game at Wembley against Newcastle – a commanding 2-0 victory.

A few months later, he was officially made club captain, and he won the FA Cup in his first season in that role. His performances to win that trophy summed Bruno up. In an amazing quarter-final at Old Trafford against Liverpool, Fernandes spent most of the game in attack, creating chances with his imagination and skill. When he suffered a small injury late on and United needed a goal to win, Bruno moved into defence, back where he played when he was a kid. Hobbling around but still running hard, he helped inspire his team-mates to a stunning 4-3 win. Then, in the final against Manchester City, he showed his attacking qualities, completing a no-look pass to assist Kobbie Mainoo's crucial goal. Everyone agreed that no other player on the pitch would have seen or tried to do the same pass. But Bruno? Well, he's our 'Portuguese magnifico'!

TROPHY HAUL

x1 FA Cup: 2024

x1 League Cup: 2023

BRUNO FERNANDES

MAGIC MOMENT

In August 2021, United played old rivals Leeds in a first Premier League game for 20 years. In front of a capacity Old Trafford crowd, following a season of mainly behind-closed-doors matches, Bruno made sure it was a memorable day by scoring a fantastic hat-trick. His first was a left-foot finish too powerful for the goalkeeper to keep out, his second another left-foot strike after cutting inside his marker, and his third was the pick of the bunch – a stunning right-footed half-volley high into the net.

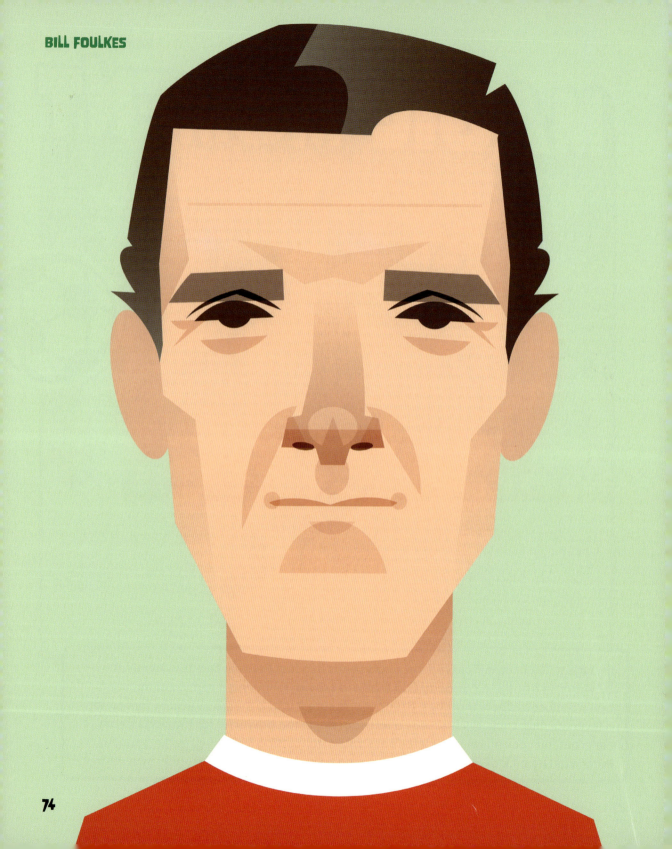

'THE DEFENSIVE ROCK'
BILL FOULKES

How a coal miner chose football over rugby to become a true club servant and help the Reds rise to the top of English and European football...

Manchester United famously became the first English club to lift the European Cup in May 1968 and in the team that night were two players who had survived the Munich Air Disaster: Bobby Charlton and William 'Bill' Anthony Foulkes. Sir Bobby's greatness has featured in a previous Heroes section, so here's the story of his team-mate...

Bill Foulkes was born in St Helens in January 1932, coming from a family of rugby league players – his grandfather captained St Helens! But it was football not rugby that Bill loved, with him representing his local side Whiston Boys Club before moving to United aged 18. The tall defender, who combined playing right-back at weekends with working as a

Foulkes started out as a right-back but later moved to centre-half where he became the enforcer in Busby's great team of the 1960s.

What a week Bill had in 1954! In the space of three days he did a shift down the mine, played his only game for England (in a 2-0 win in Northern Ireland), then flew back home to work another shift down the mine!

Foulkes finally gave up working for the coal board after playing for his country, believing if he was good enough to represent England then a career in football was achievable.

He was powerful in the air and a strong tackler, always keeping it simple with his passing... well, wouldn't you with Best, Law and Charlton in your team?

BILL FOULKES

Having survived the Munich air crash, Bill was given the captain's armband when a patched-up Reds returned to action against Sheffield Wednesday just 13 days after the accident. Ten years later he became a European Cup winner (above, right).

coal miner in between, would go on to enjoy one of the finest careers in United's history. Bill became a trainee in March 1950, signed a part-time contract with the Reds in August 1951, then made his first-team debut in December 1952.

After two appearances in 1952/53, he became a regular the following season as a wave of young players replaced the established older stars. Journalists famously nicknamed the young new players the 'Busby Babes'. Some believed top-level football in England was too tough for players still in their teens and early twenties, but Busby and his brilliant assistant Jimmy Murphy disagreed... and they were soon proven right. With stars like Tommy Taylor, Duncan Edwards and Liam Whelan, the Babes were playing exciting, attacking football. Fans flocked to see them, and they eventually raced to the First Division title in both 1955/56 and 1956/57. It meant Foulkes had two league championship winner's medals – but, sadly, he missed out on winning the '57 FA Cup, and a rare 'Double', due to defeat by Aston Villa at Wembley.

Foulkes was part of the Babes side that entered the European Cup in 1956/57,

BILL FOULKES

FRED'S FACTS!

688
Bill finished his Reds career on this many appearances – his best tally in one season was a huge 60, in 1964/65.

9
Foulkes rarely scored – his job was to stop the opposition – but he did score a goal in the Bernabeu!

1
Only the one England cap for Bill, but it was at United where he was most comfortable and valued.

becoming the first English club to take part in the competition. United beat Anderlecht (which included a record-breaking 10-0 victory!), Borussia Dortmund and Athletic Club of Bilbao, but lost 5-3 on aggregate in the semi-finals to holders and eventual winners Real Madrid.

A year older and wiser, and English champions again, the Babes went back into Europe in 1957/58 and again reached the semi-finals. Sadly, fate intervened. Having defeated Shamrock Rovers, Dukla Prague and Red Star Belgrade, the United plane crashed on the way back from Serbia after a refuelling stop in Munich. Eight players were killed, 23 people in total, with Bill one of the nine players to survive.

One of the most famous photographs in our history is the image of new captain Foulkes leading out the United team for the first game after the air crash, for an FA Cup tie against Sheffield Wednesday at Old Trafford. The new-look Reds won

BILL FOULKES

that game 3-0 and somehow made it all the way to Wembley – only for Bolton Wanderers to win the Cup final 2-0.

A rebuilding process took place, with Foulkes moving from right-back to centre-half, but it was not until 1963 that the Reds next won a trophy, defeating Leicester City 3-1 in the FA Cup final. Two years later, Busby's thrilling new team were back at the top of English football – pipping Leeds to the 1964/65 league title with superstars Denis Law, Bobby Charlton and the exciting young George Best leading the way. Another league title arrived in 1967, but it was the 'holy grail' of the European Cup that the Reds wanted most.

Ten years after Munich the dream was finally realised. United defeated Hibernians of Malta, Sarajevo, Gornik

TROPHY HAUL

x4 — First Division: 1955/56, 1956/57, 1964/65, 1966/67

x1 — FA Cup: 1963

x1 — European Cup: 1968

x3 — Charity Shield: 1956, 1957, 1967 (shared)

BILL FOULKES

MAGIC MOMENT

His strength was stopping goals, but one he scored was crucial. It came in the Bernabeu against Real Madrid in our European Cup semi-final second leg in May 1968. Having pushed forward more than usual, the big centre-half turned in a George Best cross for a 3-3 draw on the night, and 4-3 aggregate win, for a place in the Wembley final.

Zabrze and Real Madrid to reach the final at Wembley. And on a swelteringly hot night, Busby's side defeated Benfica 4-1 after extra-time. For Busby, Charlton and Foulkes, survivors of the crash, it was a poignant evening of celebrating success but remembering lost team-mates.

Not all Reds legends are international stars who excelled for their country – Foulkes won one cap for England in 1954. Some made their name because of what they achieved with their club. By the time Foulkes played his final Reds game in August 1969, he'd amassed 688 matches and scored nine goals, meaning only three players have pulled on our famous shirt more times than this undoubted United great.

'THE RECORD-BREAKER'
RYAN GIGGS

Nobody has played more times for United than the Welsh-born, Salford-bred winger-cum-midfielder – and what a player he was for the Reds over 23 years...

If you were even to dream about having a career like Ryan Giggs, you would wake up laughing with disbelief. Let the numbers explain: almost 1,000 appearances for Manchester United, 13 Premier League titles, repeated spells as a European and world champion... you get the picture. Giggsy spent his entire playing career on the books at Old Trafford and, over the course of 23 years in the United first team, he enjoyed a level of success which is almost certain to remain unbeaten.

From the moment he caught United's attention at 13, Ryan was destined to make it big with the Reds. Club legend Sir Bobby Charlton once recalled his first glimpse of watching the young winger in action during

Giggsy was the first United player to gain a mention in an episode of animated comedy The Simpsons. The same honour was later bestowed upon David Beckham and Cristiano Ronaldo!

Having featured in both the 1999 and 2008 Champions League finals, against Bayern Munich and Chelsea respectively, Giggs is the only United player in club history to have played in two successful UCL finals.

In 2010, Giggsy received the Freedom of the City of Salford for his career achievements, describing it as: "Amongst the greatest honours I have ever received."

Upon taking interim charge of United in 2014, Ryan became just the second Welshman to manage the Reds – following on from Jimmy Murphy in 1957/58.

RYAN GIGGS

Giggs celebrates his famous winning goal against Arsenal in the 1999 FA Cup semi-final replay, keeping the Reds on course for the Treble of Premier League, FA Cup and Champions League (above, right).

a training session. "I knew instantly he was simply one of those unique players," said Charlton. "I realised that although he was not a big star yet, he was definitely destined to become one. Ryan was just sensational and could see everything out on the pitch. He was always aware of what was going on around him and was never afraid to take defenders on. He always attacked the opposition."

Those characteristics were gracing senior pitches by the time Giggs was 17. The 1991/92 and 1992/93 campaigns, his first full seasons in the first team, both ended with him winning the PFA Young Player of the Year award, plus major honours: the Reds' first-ever success in the League Cup, and further glory in the newly formed Premier League.

Despite his tender years, Ryan was a crucial part of Alex Ferguson's side as soon as he was involved. His ferocious pace, unpredictable dribbling and mature understanding of the game

RYAN GIGGS

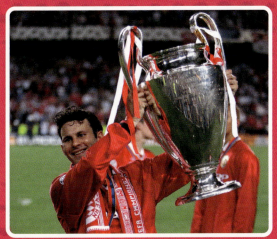

FRED'S FACTS!

963
Giggs is top of the list when it comes to United appearances – will this record ever be broken?

168
Ryan also ranks highly for goals, with some of them among the best ever scored for the Reds.

64
The Welshman represented his country this many times, and scored 12 goals along the way.

were all incredibly developed, making him a nightmarish opponent for defenders. "When he first came into the team, he was a flying machine," said team-mate Mal Donaghy. "I saw defenders try to hack him down and he was just too quick for them!"

The youngster, by that stage a full Welsh international, had also developed the handy knack of scoring regularly. He posted a career-best haul of 17 goals – an astonishing figure for a winger at the time – in 1993/94 as United went on to win a Premier League and FA Cup Double for the first time in club history.

As the years went by, so too did the milestones and the honours. Another Double in 1995/96, the Treble in 1998/99, three straight Premier League titles by the end of 2000/01 and, just when it looked like the flow was slowing down, Sir Alex began blending in the top young talents of Wayne Rooney and Cristiano Ronaldo to his experienced side. This allowed him to use Giggs more strategically after the

RYAN GIGGS

MAGIC MOMENT

In a career scattered with the highest of highs, perhaps the peak of Giggsy's time with the Reds came in Moscow in 2008, when he not only became the club's all-time leading appearance-maker, but also won the Champions League for the second time as United beat Chelsea. Not a bad night, eh?

Welshman began approaching his mid-thirties, often fielding him in central midfield, where his football intellect allowed him to adapt comfortably.

The result? In 2006/07, Giggsy set a national record with his ninth league title as the Reds saw off the challenge of Jose Mourinho's Chelsea but, in typical fashion, he was far from finished. On the day United retained the title in May 2008, Ryan scored the title-clinching second goal in a 2-0 win at Wigan and then, for good measure, broke United's all-time appearances record with his next appearance: the Champions League final win over Chelsea.

While that might have seemed like a perfect fairytale ending to any career, Giggs instead carried on without even contemplating stopping. In 2008/09,

RYAN GIGGS

as United won a third straight title, he picked up the PFA Players' Player of the Year award, then went on to add another two titles to his total, in 2010/11 and 2012/13, to clock up a frankly ludicrous 13 Premier Leagues – half of his overall haul of 26 major honours.

Giggs took on a role as player-coach under David Moyes in 2013 and then, after the Scot's dismissal, took charge as interim manager for the final four games of the season. During that run, he made his 963rd and final appearance as a United player before confirming his retirement. "I'd like to be remembered, first and foremost, as the footballer who loved playing for United," he said. Sure enough, that love was more than mutual.

TROPHY HAUL

x13
Premier League: 1992/93, 1993/94, 1995/96, 1996/97, 1998/99, 1999/2000, 2000/01, 2002/03, 2006/07, 2007/08, 2008/09, 2010/11, 2012/13

x2
Champions League: 1999, 2008

x4
FA Cup: 1994, 1996, 1999, 2004

x4
League Cup: 1992, 2006, 2009, 2010

x9
Charity/Community Shield: 1993, 1994, 1996, 1997, 2003, 2007, 2008, 2010, 2013

x1
Intercontinental Cup: 1999

x1
European Super Cup: 1991

x1
Club World Cup: 2008

MARK HUGHES

'THE WELSH WARRIOR'
MARK HUGHES

We recall the Reds career of battling Welsh forward 'Sparky' — a scorer of spectacular goals and a man who regularly came good for the big occasion…

With his brute strength and tree-trunk thighs, Mark Hughes was a formidable forward who so many defenders of the 1980s and '90s would pick out whenever asked to name their 'toughest opponent'. Hughes played for seven clubs, but most of his success came with the Reds, where he was adored by the fans.

Born in Wrexham, the Welshman joined our youth system aged 14, then signed pro at 16, after a Reds' talent scout saw him in action and was blown away by the qualities that would become his trademarks: holding up the ball with his back to goal, and those ferocious volleys that you really didn't want to get in the way of!

His full name is Leslie Mark Hughes, but he's only ever been known as Mark. 'Leslie' was so he could have his dad's name on his birth certificate.

Nobody has scored more goals for United at Wembley than Sparky, who netted six times in his 13 visits to the national stadium.

The team Hughes scored most often against for United was Coventry City, against whom he struck 10 goals.

In 1994, Hughes became only the second player — after Norman Whiteside in 1983 — to score in the finals of the FA Cup and League Cup in the same season.

MARK HUGHES

Hughes celebrates scoring against Crystal Palace in the 1990 FA Cup final, and he was always United's man for the most important games in his two spells with the Reds.

Much like his teenage team-mate Norman Whiteside, Hughes could handle the physical side of the game from a young age, with experienced pros regularly bouncing off him as they tried (and failed) to win the ball back.

Affectionately known as 'Sparky' since the aged of eight – *Sparky* was a popular kids' comic in the 1970s (which kind of rhymed with 'Mark') – Hughes made his first-team debut for the Reds in 1983, aged 19, and he'd go on to score 47 goals in 121 games during this first spell at the club, while setting up countless goals for others thanks to his hard work.

United fans were gutted when he left for Barcelona in 1986 – to partner Gary Lineker – but £2 million was a big transfer fee back then, and thankfully he'd be back two years later (for a club-record £1.8m) following an impressive loan spell away from Barça with Bayern Munich.

By that time, Alex Ferguson was United boss, and what incredible success Hughes would have under the Scotsman over the next seven seasons: two league titles, two FA Cups (to go with one from his first spell) and one League Cup in

MARK HUGHES

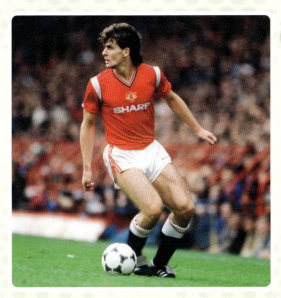

England, as well as one Cup Winners' Cup and a Super Cup in Europe.

While Sparky finished as United's top scorer in six of his 10 seasons as a Red, it was the quality of his strikes which really excited fans, with thumping volleys and powerful strikes becoming his hallmarks.

For many of United's trophy successes in this era, Hughes played a central role – be it his double in the 1990 FA Cup final against Palace, another double (including an amazing winner from a tight angle) to beat his old club Barça in the 1991 Cup Winners' Cup final, or his crashing volley in the final seconds of the 1994 FA Cup semi-final v Oldham to keep our Double dream alive. It saw Sparky build a reputation as a 'big-game player', who stepped up when it mattered most.

This was recognised by his fellow footballers, who twice voted Hughes PFA Players' Player of the Year, in 1989

FRED'S FACTS!

467
Hughes enjoyed two spells with the Reds and gave absolutely everything each time he pulled on the shirt.

163
This is Sparky's impressive goal count, but it was the quality and importance of his strikes that really stood out.

72
The Wrexham-born striker played many times for his country (scoring 16 times) and was later their manager.

MARK HUGHES

and 1991, to go with his PFA Young Player of the Year trophy from 1985. And United fans showed their appreciation too, by voting him the club's Player of the Year twice – in 1984/85 and 1990/91.

Hughes was still a regular in the United team by the time he left for Chelsea in 1995 – he played 46 times for the Reds in 1994/95 – but with a new crop of stars coming through for Ferguson (the so-called 'Class of '92'), Mark decided to join the team he supported as a kid. Further spells at Southampton, Everton and Blackburn Rovers followed, before he became Wales manager in 1999 then moved into club management in 2004. But it's for his rampaging role as a forward for United and Wales that he will always be best remembered.

TROPHY HAUL

- x2 Premier League: 1992/93, 1993/94
- x3 FA Cup: 1985, 1990, 1994
- x1 League Cup: 1992
- x3 Charity Shield: 1990 (shared), 1993, 1994
- x1 European Cup Winners' Cup: 1991
- x1 European Super Cup: 1991

MARK HUGHES

MAGIC MOMENT

His second goal against Barcelona brought the Reds a first piece of European silverware since 1968! And what a goal! He'd already scored in the 1991 Rotterdam final, applying a final touch to a Steve Bruce header, then ran on to Bryan Robson's chipped through ball to round the Barça keeper and blast into the net from the tightest of angles.

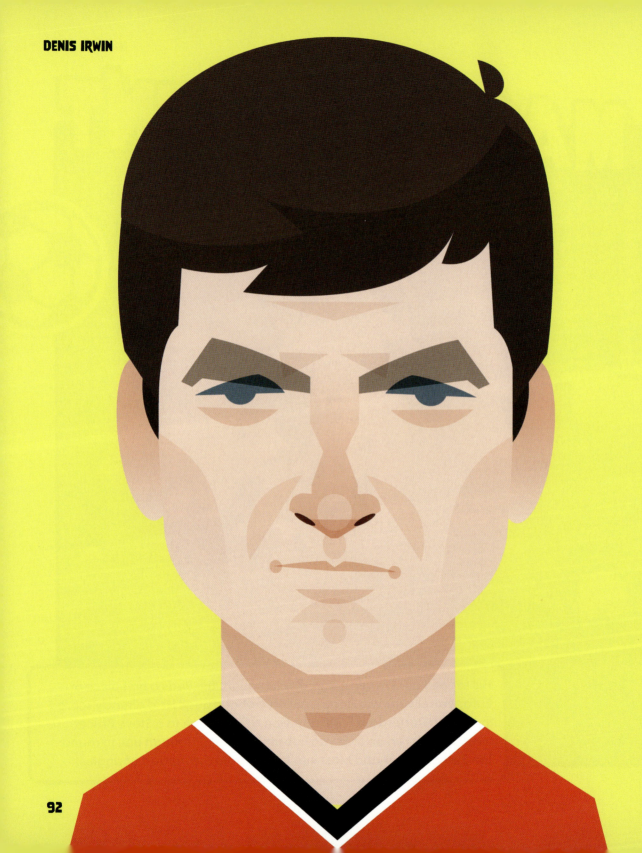

'MR DEPENDABLE'
DENIS IRWIN

A perfect professional who didn't seek the limelight, the Irishman quietly became one of the most successful players in Premier League history...

When Sir Alex Ferguson was once asked to name his greatest ever United team made up from all the players he worked with at Old Trafford, he said there was only one player guaranteed a place in the team. Who do you think that might be... the megastar Cristiano Ronaldo? The ultimate captain Roy Keane? Goalscoring genius Wayne Rooney? Nope on all three counts. The player he said would walk into his greatest side was defender Denis Irwin.

There have been many, many more glamorous or famous footballers who have pulled on the United shirt over the last 40 years, but few were as important or reliable as the Irishman, who quietly penned his name in the club's history books.

Irwin's first club in England was our old rivals Leeds — he moved over from his home in County Cork in 1983. In total he played for four teams in England: Leeds, Oldham, United and Wolves.

Denis was designated penalty-taker for the Reds for a while and netted 12 times from the spot for United.

When it comes to trophies, Denis is the joint-most successful Irish footballer ever. And do you know who he shares the record with? His old team-mate Roy Keane!

Irwin was made United captain for his final Reds appearance — his 529th! — against Charlton on 11 May 2002.

DENIS IRWIN

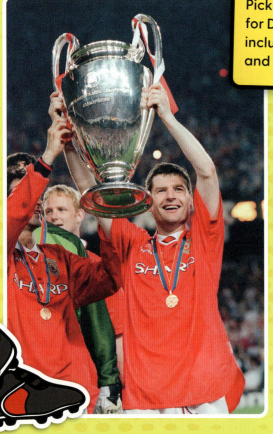

Picking up winner's medals became a real habit for Denis across his 12 seasons with United, including the Champions League in 1999 (left) and Premier League (right), on seven occasions.

The first of over 500 appearances for United happened in August 1990, against Liverpool in the Charity Shield at Wembley. He had signed for the Reds that summer, having impressed Alex Ferguson in the FA Cup semi-final playing against United for Oldham Athletic, who took us to a replay before we finally triumphed on the way to Sir Alex's first trophy as United manager. Denis was an instant success in the Reds' defence, playing 52 games and lifting a trophy at the end of his very first season – the European Cup Winners' Cup v Barcelona.

His importance for the side really became clear when we lifted the first ever Premier League title in 1993 as he played every match in that championship-winning campaign, and he did even better the next season when we won the club's first league and FA Cup Double in 1994 – Irwin was the only player in the squad to play every single game in both the league and Cup. Great effort, Den!

That was just one of the reasons Ferguson loved Irwin – he was always available and rarely injured, and when he did play he barely made a mistake or let the side down. And for a defender, he scored way more than his fair share of goals. He struck 33 times in total for United – he was brilliant from the penalty spot but also smashed in some amazing, unstoppable free-kicks!

Like many of his team-mates, the high point of Irwin's United career was the unforgettable Treble campaign of 1998/99. Frustratingly he was suspended for the FA Cup final against Newcastle, having been sent off against Liverpool, but he returned for the Champions League final against Bayern Munich to join in the glory after maybe our ultimate 'Fergie time' victory! Denis continued to play an important role for the Reds, but

DENIS IRWIN

FRED'S FACTS!

529
Not only was Denis reliable on the pitch, but he was always available to play – hence this huge games total.

33
There aren't many goalscoring full-backs around, but Irwin was definitely one of the first!

56
The proud Irishman won this many caps for his country, and was in their USA '94 World Cup squad.

by the end of the 2001/02 season, his games were becoming fewer as the years caught up with him, and with new signing Mikael Silvestre taking his left-back slot more and more often. His last game for United came when he was 36, at home to Charlton Athletic in May 2002.

But Denis's career wasn't over yet. He signed for Championship side Wolves that summer and when his new club were promoted to the Premier League, it meant he got to come back and play at Old Trafford one last time, where he was

DENIS IRWIN

MAGIC MOMENT

A goal every 16 games (on average) was a healthy return for a full-back, and the most vital of his strikes came in the final weeks of 1992/93, away to Coventry City. Irwin's 40th-minute shot from outside the box went low into the net for a 1-0 win, keeping up momentum as the Reds finally ended a 26-year wait for the league title.

DENIS IRWIN

given a hero's reception by thousands of United fans. And no wonder... during his 12 seasons in the famous red shirt he won an incredible 18 trophies.

Since retiring, Denis has been a regular face at Old Trafford where he often hosts in the hospitality suites and speaks on MUTV. And wherever he goes inside the ground, fans will always shake his hand and thank him for all he did for United. And no wonder... Denis, you're a legend!

TROPHY HAUL

x7

Premier League:
1992/93, 1993/94, 1995/96, 1996/97, 1998/99, 1999/2000, 2000/01

x1

Champions League:
1999

x2

FA Cup:
1994, 1996

x1

League Cup:
1992

x4

Charity Shield:
1990 (shared), 1993, 1996, 1997

x1

European Cup Winners' Cup:
1991

x1

Intercontinental Cup:
1999

x1

European Super Cup:
1991

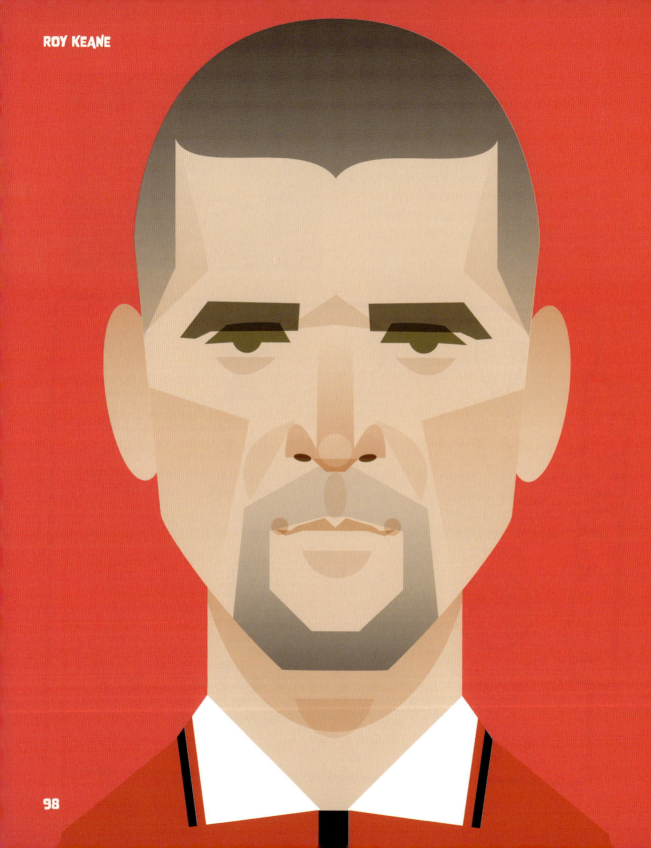

'KEANO'
ROY KEANE

As tough-as-nails in midfield, no opponent enjoyed going up against the intimidating Irishman, who wore the shirt (and so often the armband) for a dozen incredible years...

You've no doubt seen Roy Keane as a pundit on TV (usually providing great entertainment with his outspoken views!) but between 1997 and 2005 he was the most successful captain Manchester United have ever had.

Keane, you see, had a way of bringing out the very best in his team-mates – a proper 'midfield general' who would do anything to protect his fellow troops in the red shirts.

Yes, he did sometimes see red too – he was sent off a club-record 11 times, to be precise! – but he did play nearly 500 games for us, and he always gave everything for his team. The fans loved him for that, and 'Keano! Keano!' would regularly ring around the stands of Old Trafford – and still does!

Roy was oustanding for United in 1999/2000, being voted Footballer of the Year, PFA Players' Player of the Year, and Sir Matt Busby Player of the Year!

As a youngster, Keane took up boxing and even had four bouts in the Irish Novice League – winning all four of his fights.

Although Reds fans always called him 'Keano', his nickname in the United dressing room was actually 'Keanie'.

Roy's 2006 testimonial between United and Celtic was a full house at Old Trafford – 69,591 – which is the largest crowd for a testimonial in England.

ROY KEANE

Roy loved a midfield battle, and the United skipper enjoyed plenty of them with Arsenal's Patrick Vieira. Reds fans voted Roy their Player of the Year in both 1999 and 2000 (right).

Roy Maurice Keane looked like a natural leader from the first time he kicked a ball for his local team in Cork, Ireland, in the 1980s, and his favourite player growing up was Bryan Robson – another box-to-box midfielder and United's captain at the time. Little did young Roy know that one day they'd be winning a Double together, but not before Roy had spent three excellent years with Nottingham Forest.

It was summer 1993 when Keane swapped Forest, where he'd played under their legendary manager Brian Clough, for Alex Ferguson's Reds. The £3.75 million fee was a British record (how things have changed since then!) and although Roy would have to wait a few years to become captain – Robson, Steve Bruce, then Eric Cantona each wearing the armband before him – the Irishman was a key part of the team from day one.

After the Reds' first-ever Premier League and FA Cup Double in 1993/94, we'd win it again in 1995/96… and incredibly we'd go

ROY KEANE

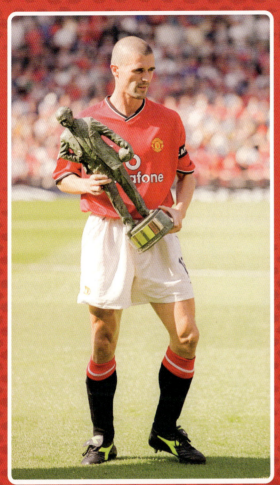

FRED'S FACTS!

480
Not only did Keano play this many times for United, but he was also club captain for eight years.

51
Roy's influence on the team wasn't measured in goals, but he still made an important goal contribution.

67
Keane took playing for Ireland very seriously, winning this many caps and scoring nine goals.

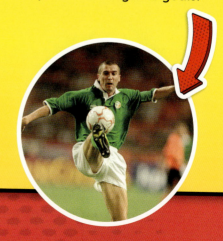

one better than that in 1998/99, as United became the first English team to win the Treble of the league title, FA Cup and Champions League.

As club captain, Keane played 55 games in that Treble season, although sadly he'd miss the Champions League final against Bayern Munich through suspension. But if it wasn't for Roy we almost certainly wouldn't have made it to that final in Barcelona, after he produced one of the all-time great performances

ROY KEANE

MAGIC MOMENT

His captain's display at Juventus in the Champions League semi-final second leg in April 1999 is the stuff of legend. Despite knowing he was going to miss the final after picking up a yellow card, Roy doubled his efforts, scored and bossed the midfield as the Reds claimed a place in the Nou Camp final.

ROY KEANE

from a United player in the semi-final. Two goals down away to Juventus in Turin, Italy, he dragged his team back into it with a thumping header, and our opponents just couldn't stop Keane bossing the midfield as the Reds fought back to a stunning 3-2 victory (and 4-3 on aggregate).

Roy would go on to captain United to many more trophies – he'd even score the winner when we were crowned the best team on the planet in late 1999 by winning the Intercontinental Cup – but it's his passion on the pitch that he's best remembered for: be it that amazing display against Juventus, his intense rivalry with certain opponents (such as Arsenal's Patrick Vieira), or those rocket goals of his – hard and low into the bottom corner of the net. There's only one Keano!

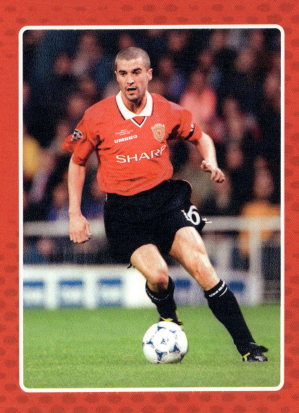

 TROPHY HAUL

 x7
Premier League: 1993/94, 1995/96, 1996/97, 1998/99, 1999/2000, 2000/01, 2002/03

 x1
Champions League: 1999

 x4
FA Cup: 1994, 1996, 1999, 2004

x4
Charity/Community Shield: 1993, 1996, 1997, 2003

 x1
Intercontinental Cup: 1999

'THE KING' DENIS LAW

Our Scottish scorer supreme was as prolific as any striker on the planet throughout the 1960s, and he's now immortalised as part of the 'United Trinity'...

Ask your parents about the king of the Stretford End and they'll probably tell you stories of Eric Cantona. But then ask your grandparents the same thing and you'll likely get a very different answer. That's because, for Reds fans who lived through the 1960s, there is only one true king of Old Trafford... and they'll tell you his name is Denis Law.

There's a good chance you'll walk past 'The Lawman' whenever you visit the stadium, as he's immortalised in bronze alongside his fellow Sixties icons George Best and Sir Bobby Charlton. The United Trinity statue on the main forecourt is dedicated to three of the four players to win the *Ballon d'Or* while with the Reds (the other being Cristiano Ronaldo), and

Law holds the club record for most hat-tricks. He picked up the matchball 18 times for United — four of those being four-goal hauls!

Sir Bobby Charlton famously said of his team-mate: "The public absolutely loved him. They couldn't take their eyes off him. There were times when he was simply unstoppable."

The Trinity statue is not the only one of Denis at Old Trafford — there's another of him in the Stretford End tier two concourse.

The day after United had won the European Cup in 1968, manager Busby visited injured Denis in hospital with the trophy — so much better than a bunch of flowers!

DENIS LAW

King of the continent: Denis is presented with the 1964 *Ballon d'Or* on the Old Trafford pitch, two years after being handed a debut – and a red shirt! (above, right) – by Matt Busby in 1962, against West Brom (he scored).

amazingly all three came from the same all-conquering United team.

Scotsmen have played a huge part in the history of the Reds – most famously managers Sir Matt Busby and Sir Alex Ferguson – and Denis is another club legend from north of the border. He was born in Aberdeen in 1940, the youngest of seven children to his mother Robina and his father George. His dad was a fisherman, but Denis only ever wanted to be a footballer.

At the age of 15, he moved to England and signed amateur forms for Huddersfield Town. He made his debut in December 1956 and soon thrived under Terriers boss Bill Shankly (who would later famously manage Liverpool). After being capped for Scotland in October 1958 – for whom he'd score 30 goals from 55 appearances – he moved to Manchester City in a British record £55,000 move in March 1960. His stay at the Blues was short, moving to Torino in Italy in summer 1961. Law performed well in *Serie A* – scoring 10 goals – but struggled to settle.

United boss Busby had tried to sign Law from Huddersfield years earlier but finally

DENIS LAW

FRED'S FACTS!

404
Injuries and suspensions occasionally kept the Scotsman out of action, but his games total for United is still huge!

237
Only Wayne Rooney (253) and Bobby Charlton (249) have scored more times for United than Law!

55
This is how many caps the proud Aberdonian won for Scotland, scoring 30 goals. Lethal!

got his man in July 1962, bringing him to Old Trafford for £115,000. He scored seven minutes into his debut, against West Bromwich Albion, and then the goals kept on flowing. He was part of the Reds' FA Cup success against Leicester City in 1963, scoring our first goal in a 3-1 Wembley win. And he ended that first season with 29 goals in 44 appearances.

If he was good in his first campaign, then he was unstoppable in his second. In 1963/64 he fired a (still) club record 46 goals from just 42 matches, a total that included seven hat-tricks! Sadly, that contribution was not enough to help United to win trophies, but it did earn him the 1964 *Ballon d'Or* award – given to European football's best player.

A year later, he was the First Division's top scorer with 28 goals (39 in all competitions) as United won the 1964/65 First Division title ahead of Leeds. It was

DENIS LAW

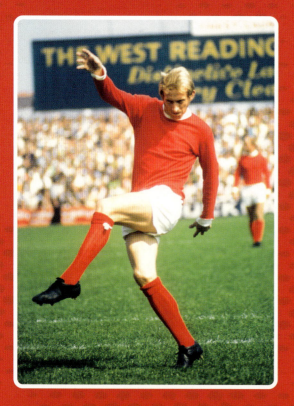

the Reds' first title since the Munich Air Disaster, with the next arriving in 1966/67. Law was the undoubted leader of United's forward line, and club captain, but he wasn't the only superstar for the Reds. Alongside him in an awesome attack were England World Cup winner and 1966 *Ballon d'Or* holder Bobby Charlton, and another of the game's greatest ever players, George Best. The 'Trinity', as they became known, terrorised defences across Europe.

Law was prolific in the air and with both feet, and his match-winning flashes of genius made him a menace for defences. Add in a fierce hunger to win with incredible bravery, and it's no wonder he was nicknamed 'the king' by United fans. His importance to Matt Busby's brilliant team also made him a target for

x2
First Division: 1964/65, 1966/67

x1
European Cup: 1968

x1
FA Cup: 1963

x2
Charity Shield: 1965 (shared), 1967 (shared)

x1
Ballon d'Or: 1964

DENIS LAW

MAGIC MOMENT

Law was the master of magic moments, often producing something surprising to turn a game United's way. Like in the 1963 FA Cup final when he scored the opening goal – taking a pass with his left foot, swivelling on to his right and firing home. It teed up a 3-1 win as the Reds lifted the Cup!

opposition defenders, and he suffered plenty of bumps across his career. Sadly, one such injury kept him out of the 1968 European Cup final win against Benfica at Wembley; he watched our 4-1 victory on TV in hospital after a knee operation.

He returned the following season to score 30 goals in 1968/69, but injuries continued to hamper him. Denis moved to Manchester City in summer 1973 on a free transfer, having scored 237 goals from 404 matches. While Denis will forever remain part of the United Trinity, he will also be remembered as one of a kind: a ferocious goal-getting machine.

BILLY MEREDITH

'THE WELSH WIZARD'
BILLY MEREDITH

Not many players are heroes at both United and City, but this man was! Meet one of football's first superstars, who lined up for us over 100 years ago...

What do Peter Schmeichel, Carlos Tevez, Denis Law, Owen Hargreaves and Andy Cole have in common? That's right, they all played for both Manchester clubs – and there are plenty more on that list, including one man at the very start who you might not know too much about: William Henry Meredith.

If Billy – as he was better known – had been born a few decades later he'd be a household name even now, but Welshman Meredith kicked a ball (a heavy one at that!) in a very different era, playing over 700 games for City and United either side of the First World War, between 1894 and 1924. He was as famous as footballers came back then,

Billy's position was 'outside forward' – basically a winger, although many teams played with five forwards back then, making today's wingers look quite defensive!

Meredith holds the record as United's oldest ever player – he was 46 years and 281 days old when he appeared against Derby County in May 1921.

The Welshman was a founder member of what became the Professional Footballers Association, even going on strike to help players' rights.

Billy lived until the age of 83, passing away in April 1958, two months after the Munich Air Disaster.

BILLY MEREDITH

Billy keeps the ball in play, and launches into another attack, against Queens Park Rangers in the 1908 Charity Shield.

though, especially in Manchester, where he helped City and United win their first trophies, while he still holds records with both clubs over a century later.

Born near Wrexham, Wales, Billy worked at a coal mine while playing for his local side Chirk, before crossing the border into England to join Northwich Victoria in 1892. He was still a teenager then, but already he was wowing the crowds with his amazing dribbling down the wing, usually followed by either an accurate cross or a lethal shot. Manchester City were one of the teams Billy faced, and in 1894 he joined them – although only as an amateur, meaning he could still live at home and work in the pit, which kept his mum very happy!

In November 1894, he played for City in the first Manchester league derby, scoring twice. Thankfully we won 5-2, but his performance caught the attention of the United staff, as well as the fans, and by the age of 20 Meredith had turned

BILLY MEREDITH

FRED'S FACTS!

335
Billy's games total came across three competitions: the league, FA Cup and Charity Shield.

36
His main job was tricking his way past defenders to supply the strikers, but he scored roughly every nine games.

48
This is his cap count for Wales, a very impressive total at a time of fewer international matches.

professional and was already playing for Wales. Over the next 12 seasons he'd become City's star man as they won the Second Division in 1899, then the FA Cup in 1904 – City's first major trophies. But after Meredith was caught up in a financial scandal at City in 1906, he knew the opportunity to move to the other side of Manchester would free him up to start playing again and earning money.

Super-fit and healthy off the pitch (unlike many players back then!), he was

BILLY MEREDITH

MAGIC MOMENT

Having helped Manchester City to win their first trophies, Billy moved to United and, as one of the star players, helped Ernest Mangnall's Reds do the same. The moustachioed Meredith is pictured here – sat between the Charity Shield and the First Division trophy – with his United team-mates following their 1908 triumphs.

rarely injured and could keep on running, often while chewing on a toothpick to help him focus! Sounds dangerous, yes, but such was his fantastic balance, he was rarely knocked off his feet.

Billy would spend 11 seasons at United, and once again he'd play a key role in his team winning trophies for the first time, including the biggest prize in England in the First Division title (1908 and 1911), as well as his second FA Cup (1909). Chuck in a couple of Charity Shields (1908 and 1911), plus a first British Home Championship with Wales (1907) and no wonder he was a hero to so many. Billy was also never afraid to speak his mind, either, as he campaigned for footballers

BILLY MEREDITH

to have more rights and be paid more (they didn't earn much in those days), as well as improvements in coaching to help younger players develop ball skills as good as his! The Welshman's fearlessness to take on the English FA made him a controversial figure at times, but he always commanded respect, and when he had a benefit match in 1912, soon after his 38th birthday, 39,000 fans turned up.

Billy wasn't done there though – not even close, as he played over 100 more games over nine years for United, before his last Reds game, in May 1921, aged 46!

Time for retirement, right? Wrong! Incredibly, he then returned to City, where he made 31 more appearances, including in a derby game against United in October 1921, before Billy's brilliant boots were finally hung up for good.

x2

First Division:
1907/08, 1910/11

x1

FA Cup:
1909

x2

Charity Shield:
1908, 1911

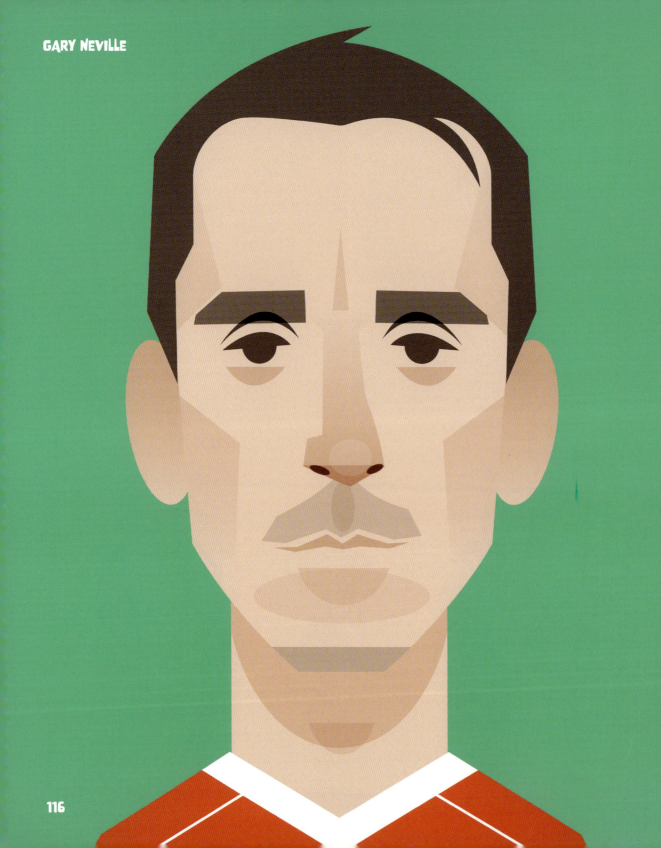

'THE LIFELONG RED'

GARY NEVILLE

Meet our Red-to-the-core right-back who went from watching from the Stretford End as a youngster to leading out United as captain – always giving his absolute all…

Upon announcing his retirement from playing in 2011, aged 35, right-back Gary Neville brought down the curtain on a career he never could have realistically imagined when growing up as a youngster who worshipped Reds captain Bryan Robson. Recognisable more recently as one of modern football's leading commentators and analysts, the Bury-born defender racked up an astonishing total of 18 major honours during one of the best defensive careers ever enjoyed at Old Trafford. By his own admission, Gary made up for any shortcomings in his natural talent by working harder than anyone else, which, in a hard-grafting team, was some effort! From a young age, he would religiously

Gary was a superb cricketer in his youth, representing Lancashire's Under-14s alongside his brother, Phil.

The Nevilles are one of 12 sets of brothers to play for United's first team and, after Phil's move to Everton, they also became the first brothers to captain opposing teams in the Premier League!

Gary's sister, Tracey, was a professional netballer who played for England. She later became their coach and guided them to gold at the 2018 Commonwealth Games.

As well as gaining post-retirement prominence as a TV commentator and pundit, Gary is also a keen entrepreneur, even being a co-owner of Salford City Football Club.

GARY NEVILLE

One of Gary's childhood heroes was United skipper Bryan Robson, and having followed him by being made club captain in 2005 he realised another dream of lifting trophies as team leader.

practise every single aspect of his game, even throw-ins. Former Reds winger Lee Sharpe once recalled hearing a thudding sound at The Cliff training ground, at which point he went outside and discovered Neville working on his throw-ins against a wall. "As hard as he could, over and over again," said Sharpe. "Practising long throws... Gary Neville's idea of fun!"

While some players might have found Neville's dedication amusing, his coaches were certainly won over. "He was working so hard to improve his ability," said famed youth-team coach Eric Harrison. "At 16, I made him the captain of the youth team. That was unusual because normally I would give the job to a 17 or 18-year-old who would be more mature. I was certain Gary would be a first-team player and an international footballer. There was no more dedicated player in football."

A vocal presence in defence, Gary's role was split between centre-back and right-back during his younger years, specialising in the latter as he broke into United's first-team set-up. Shortly after lifting the FA Youth Cup as part of the famous Class of '92, Neville debuted in Alex Ferguson's first team and, within long, began to establish himself as regular squad member. His breakthrough campaign came in 1994/95 when he

GARY NEVILLE

FRED'S FACTS!

602
Gary played a huge number of games for United – he is fifth on the club's all-time appearances list.

7
It wasn't his job to score goals, meaning that he really enjoyed it when he found the back of the net.

85
Gary was hugely proud of playing for England, and never let his country down in winning this many caps.

made 27 appearances, including the Reds' FA Cup semi-final (plus the replay) against Crystal Palace. "Getting through that game and playing well, then playing well and winning the replay; that's the point where I thought: 'I'm in here.' I felt confident," he recalled.

Over the next 12 seasons, Neville was the Reds' unquestioned starting right-back, motoring up and down the right flank non-stop, always looking to use the ball intelligently and becoming a highly reliable supplier of right-wing crosses. He was initially stationed behind Andrei Kanchelskis, then youth-team colleague and close friend David Beckham, before subsequently striking up a new relationship with a fledgling Cristiano Ronaldo. Those dozen years coincided with some of the greatest campaigns in club history at Old Trafford.

Only a serious ankle injury disrupted Gary's 2006/07 campaign, sidelining him for the run-in, but he had already done enough to earn a Premier League winner's

GARY NEVILLE

medal that term. Upon collecting it, he had reached 13 major honours, including seven league titles.

At 32, physically recovering from such a substantial injury setback took time, forcing Neville to lean on his experience and knowhow. Prior to his retirement midway through the 2010/11 campaign, he turned in a succession of key performances as the Reds continued scooping silverware, ensuring another

TROPHY HAUL

x8
Premier League: 1995/96, 1996/97, 1998/99, 1999/2000, 2000/01, 2002/03, 2006/07, 2008/09

x2
Champions League: 1999, 2008

x3
FA Cup: 1996, 1999, 2004

x3
League Cup: 2006, 2009, 2010

x3
Charity/Community Shield: 1996, 1997, 2008

x1
Intercontinental Cup: 1999

x1
Club World Cup: 2008

GARY NEVILLE

MAGIC MOMENT

As for any United fan of a certain age, 1999's Treble-clinching Champions League final against Bayern Munich represented pure heaven for Gary. "It was supernatural," he smiled afterwards. "It was like nothing I have ever experienced before in my life."

stint as a Premier League champion and Club World Cup winner before he finally hung up his boots.

As that news broke in early 2011, the tributes soon began pouring in. "Gary was the best English right-back of his generation," stressed Sir Alex Ferguson. "He is an example to any young professional; hard-working, loyal and intelligent. As a United fan born and bred, his fantastic career at Old Trafford has cemented his place in the affection of the club's supporters everywhere."

As the famous terrace chant went then, goes now and will forever be, Gary Neville is a Red.

'HOMETOWN HERO'
MARCUS RASHFORD

Raised just up the road from Old Trafford, the forward burst on to the scene in 2016, before going on to become a role model for so many kids, in Manchester and beyond...

Manchester United's Academy has been famous for a long, long time, but it still continues to produce amazing, young, talented players. Arguably our greatest youth graduate of the 21st century is Wythenshawe-born Marcus Rashford, who blasted his way to fame out of nowhere back in 2016. By the time he was 24, he had already scored 100 United goals!

Marcus's fairytale story started on a cold February night at Old Trafford in 2015/16. United were in the midst of an injury crisis, so Rashford was drafted in as a substitute for our Europa League knockout game against Midtjylland. But when Anthony Martial went down in the warm-up, the 18-year-old was handed an unexpected chance to start from

In 2020, he was awarded an MBE for his campaigning work against child poverty, which instigated a government U-turn to make sure kids received free school meals during the Covid-19 pandemic.

He is the only United player to reach 100 goals in the post-Sir Alex Ferguson era.

Along with Dennis Viollet, Rashford is the only Red in history to have scored in nine consecutive games at Old Trafford.

Marcus has an amazing record of scoring on his debuts, doing so in the Champions League, Europa League, Premier League and the League Cup!

MARCUS RASHFORD

With well over a century of goals, our hotshot no.10 has provided many celebratory moments for the Reds, including against Barcelona in the Europa League (left), a competition he helped us win in 2017 (top right).

the beginning. It was an important match: The Danish club had pulled off a shock 2-1 win in the first leg. Even worse, they opened the scoring in Manchester too, leaving us on the brink of elimination! We needed a fightback, and Rashford prompted one, with two debut goals that inspired a 5-1 victory!

Three days later, Arsenal arrived at Old Trafford in the Premier League and, again, Rashford was tasked with leading the attack. Incredibly, he repeated the feat! United won 3-2, and the precocious Mancunian netted twice within four minutes to leave the Gunners reeling.

From nowhere, Rashford had thrust himself into the headlines. By the end of his first season, he was even an FA Cup winner and an England international. Oh, and he also scored the winner in his first Manchester derby – incredible!

From that point on, Rashford became one of United's most important players. Even throughout numerous managerial changes, and the arrival of countless new strikers, our Academy hero continued to

MARCUS RASHFORD

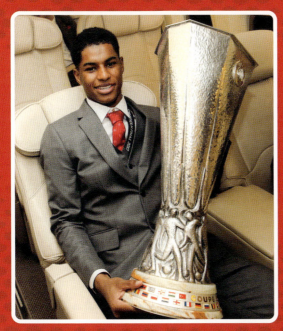

FRED'S FACTS!

402
Marcus brought up his 400th Reds game in May 2024, with his 402nd being our 2024 FA Cup final win.

131
Rashford's goal tally by the end of the 2023/24 season put him into our top 15 of all-time scorers.

60
Number of caps Marcus has won for England so far, scoring 17 goals along the way.

build a remarkable career stuffed with memorable moments. In 2018, he scored twice to help us defeat Jurgen Klopp's Liverpool at Old Trafford. The next year, he took responsibility in the Champions League when we were awarded a stoppage-time penalty against Paris Saint-Germain. Rashford's perfect spot-kick, powered past Italian goalkeeping legend Gianluigi Buffon, sealed one of the sweetest moments in the club's recent history, sending us through to the Champions League quarter-finals despite a 2-0 deficit from the first leg.

In 2019/20, he surpassed 20 goals in a season for the first time in his career (22), and also won our Goal of the Season prize for a staggering, Ronaldo-esque free-kick against Chelsea at Stamford Bridge. The following year, he notched 21, including

MARCUS RASHFORD

MAGIC MOMENT

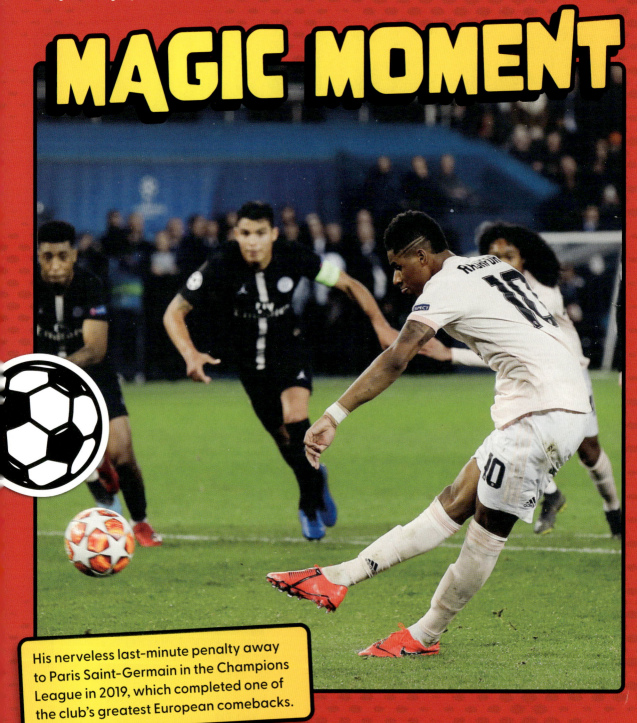

His nerveless last-minute penalty away to Paris Saint-Germain in the Champions League in 2019, which completed one of the club's greatest European comebacks.

MARCUS RASHFORD

another decisive strike against PSG and a first Champions League hat-trick, against RB Leipzig. His best season to date came in Erik ten Hag's first year as manager, when Rashford became the first United player since Robin van Persie to reach 30 goals in a single campaign. He also scored our second in the League Cup final victory over Newcastle United at Wembley. That was also the season he became just the 22nd player in club history to reach 100 goals, and the first Academy-taught player to do so since Paul Scholes.

He was a pivotal figure in our memorable 2024 FA Cup final success over Manchester City at Wembley too and, given his age, who knows what more Marcus could achieve in his career before he hangs up his boots?

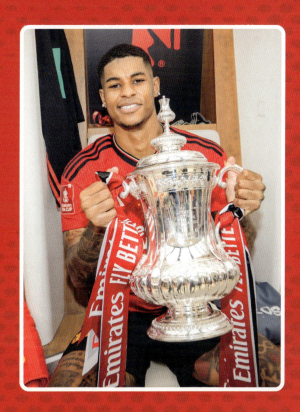

TROPHY HAUL

x2
FA Cup:
2016, 2024

x2
League Cup:
2017, 2023

x1
Europa League:
2017

x1
Community Shield:
2016

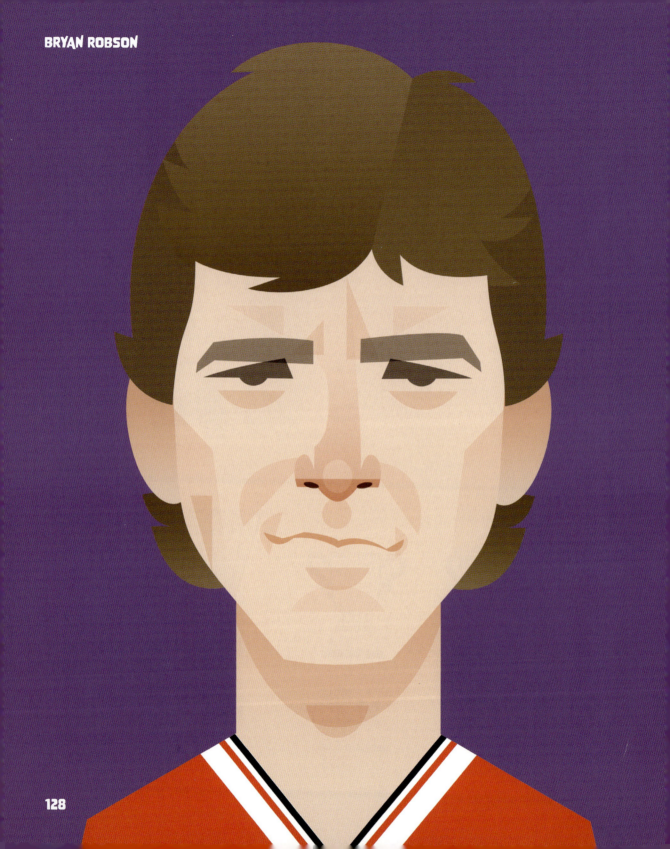

'CAPTAIN MARVEL'
BRYAN ROBSON

So courageous were this man's displays as skipper for United and England that he was given an appropriately heroic nickname! Let's revisit his career…

Ask anyone who saw the great Bryan Robson line up for United and they'll remember the all-action midfield legend getting stuck in and shouting instructions to his team-mates just like it was yesterday.

"A captain should be able to lift players when things aren't going well and give them self-belief," he once said, and from 1981 to 1994 'Robbo' seemed to do that better than anyone on the pitch, for both club and country. He had some bad luck with injuries, but even when he wasn't playing his presence as part of the squad seemed to lift everybody, which is why he remained so vital to United's first-team squad for 13 seasons.

Bryan is United's longest-serving captain, doing the job from 1982-1994, although he did share the role with Steve Bruce in his final two years.

Despite the Reds not winning any major trophies in 1983/84, Robbo was on fire, hitting a whopping 18 goals from midfield!

In 1990, Robson became the first United captain to lift the FA Cup three times — adding to his wins as skipper in 1983 and 1985.

United fans voted Robbo as the Reds' Player of the Year twice: first in 1982/83, then again in 1988/89.

BRYAN ROBSON

Welcome to United! Robson signs for the Reds on the Old Trafford pitch in October 1981, a deal sealed with a handshake from club chairman Martin Edwards.

It's fascinating to hear how many players name Robbo as being someone who inspired them when they were kids – David Beckham being one. As a teenager in the Reds' Academy, Becks made sure he got to clean Robson's boots... because he knew that would give him the chance to ask for advice and tips. Smart lad!

As a kid himself, growing up in County Durham, Robbo was captain of his school team, and when he was 15 he was approached by West Bromwich Albion, the club where he'd really start to make his name. Over 200 appearances later, Robson was a man in demand, and United boss Ron Atkinson – who had managed him before at West Brom – won the battle for his signature in 1981, for a British record transfer fee of £1.5 million.

The midfielder was soon made captain, and in 1983 he won his first trophy as our skipper, as we beat Brighton & Hove Albion in the FA Cup final. Robbo scored twice in the 4-0 replay win, and even

BRYAN ROBSON

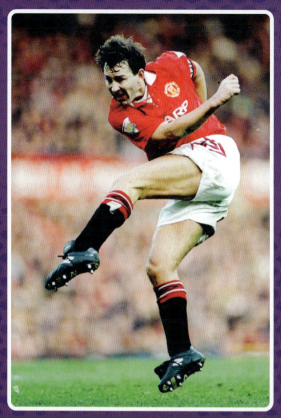

FRED'S FACTS!

461
Playing this many games is impressive, and 'Captain Marvel' gave his all in every one of them.

99
Our former skipper fell agonisingly close to a century of goals, but even a striker would be proud of this total!

90
Sixty-four of Bryan's caps for England came as captain, and he also scored 26 goals for the Three Lions.

turned down the chance to take a hat-trick-clinching penalty with the Reds 3-0 up, so that the agreed spot-kick taker Arnold Muhren could have it. Now that's top leadership!

That FA Cup final is just one of loads of highlights from Robson's United career. Be it scoring twice against Barcelona in 1984 as the Reds fought back from 0-2 down on aggregate to beat them 3-2. Or beating Barça again in the 1991 European Cup Winners' Cup final – our captain that night in Rotterdam considers this game to be his best-ever United performance. Or scoring the final goal of the Reds' 1992/93 campaign – our first

BRYAN ROBSON

league title in 26 years – with the winning goal away to Wimbledon. We could go on, as Robbo had so many brilliant memories at Old Trafford across his 13 years in the famous red shirt.

Robbo finally called time on his United career at the age of 37, after 461 games, 99 goals (so close to 100... if only he'd taken that '83 Cup final penalty!) and nine trophies (all as captain or joint-captain), to join Middlesbrough as their player-manager. By that time he'd already handed over his iconic no.7 shirt – previously worn by George Best among others – to a certain Frenchman who liked to play with his collar up. As for Beckham, who had spent so many hours shining up Robbo's boots at the training ground, one day that famous shirt would be his...

TROPHY HAUL

x2
Premier League:
1992/93, 1993/94

x3
FA Cup:
1983, 1985, 1990

x1
League Cup: 1992

x1
European Cup Winners' Cup:
1991

x2
Charity Shield:
1983, 1993

BRYAN ROBSON

MAGIC MOMENT

There are so many to choose from, but his part in our incredible 3-2 aggregate win against Barcelona in 1984 takes some beating. He was at his inspirational best, scoring twice as United overturned a 0-2 deficit from the first leg with as good a performance from a captain as you'll ever see. At full-time he was carried from the pitch on the shoulders of the fans!

'WAZZA'
WAYNE ROONEY

As the top-scoring player in club history, the forward's impact at Old Trafford will never be forgotten. And it all began with a Champions League hat-trick...

Having debuted at just 16 years of age with his boyhood team, Everton, 'Wazza' grabbed the attention of the football world by netting a last-minute screamer against champions Arsenal in October 2002. From there, he never looked back. By the end of the following season, Rooney had become the star of an England team which caught the eye at Euro 2004 and it was obvious he'd soon leave Goodison Park for a bigger club.

Over at Old Trafford, United had been aware of Rooney's talents for years, having first spotted him when he scored six times against the Reds in an Under-9s game, so Sir Alex Ferguson was desperate to sign the youngster.

It took a then-record fee for a teenager to capture Rooney, but the deal went through in

Wayne isn't the only member of his family in professional football — his brother John and cousin Tommy have both represented Macclesfield, while another cousin, Jake, has played for Derby County.

Rooney swept the boards of personal awards in 2009/10, being named PFA, Football Writers' and Sir Matt Busby Player of the Year.

As a kid Rooney used to do a bit of boxing, pulling on the gloves in his uncle's sparring gym in Croxteth. "Me being able to play in the Premier League at 16 was down to the boxing I was doing," he said. "It made me physically ready."

As an early adopter of social media, Wayne became the first Premier League footballer to reach 10 million followers on X, back when it was known as Twitter.

WAYNE ROONEY

After being unveiled at Old Trafford on 31 August 2004 (above), 18-year-old Rooney was soon into his goalscoring stride as he marked his Reds debut with a brilliant hat-trick. From then on, there was no looking back as he went on to become our all-time record goalscorer.

late August 2004. Though United fans had to be patient to get their first glimpse of him in a red shirt while he recovered from injury, he proved more than worth the wait. A month after signing, Wayne made his Reds debut in a Champions League clash with Fenerbahce at Old Trafford and promptly scored a hat-trick!

Not only did he make history as only the second debutant in club history ever to score three times in his first appearance, all three goals were absolute worldies: a left-footer into the roof of the net, a long-range right-footed thunderbolt and a top-corner free-kick… hat-tricks don't come any better than that!

"After the game, I just sat down and couldn't believe what had just happened. That was when it really hit me that I'd just scored a hat-trick on my debut," Rooney recalled. "It's a night that will always be very special to me."

Having set a high standard on day one, Wazza continued to adapt seamlessly to life at Old Trafford, netting 17 goals in his first season, 19 in his second and then 23 in his third. As he developed, United's fortunes continued to improve. Having won the League Cup in Rooney's second season, the Reds then became

WAYNE ROONEY

FRED'S FACTS!

559
Rooney played for United across 13 seasons, with only five players pulling on the red shirt more times.

253
This goal total makes Rooney our leading all-time scorer, ahead of Sir Bobby Charlton on 249.

120
And what an incredible haul of caps for his country, with Wayne scoring 53 times for the Three Lions.

Premier League champions in his third and began dominating English football's major honours. Three straight league titles arrived between 2006/07 and 2008/09, with the Champions League and Club World Cup thrown into the mix in 2008, and Rooney was at the heart of it all. Whether operating as a striker or from a wide position, his football intelligence and raw power made him an unstoppable opponent.

The departure of Cristiano Ronaldo in the summer of 2009 changed the demands on Rooney, who was soon required to focus on scoring as many goals as possible, rather than having a huge role in United's build-up play. He met those demands spectacularly, scoring a career-best 34 goals in both 2009/10 and 2011/12, establishing himself as one of the deadliest goalscorers in world football. He also took on more responsibility as his Reds career developed, and he was named club captain by new manager Louis van Gaal in

WAYNE ROONEY

MAGIC MOMENT

Despite all the trophies and his historic debut, Wazza will always be best remembered for his incredible overhead kick against Manchester City in February 2011. The iconic effort – remarkably similar to Alejandro Garnacho's 2023 stunner at Everton – was voted the greatest goal of the Premier League's first 20 seasons.

WAYNE ROONEY

2014, a role he retained for his final three seasons at the club.

During his last campaign, 2016/17, Wayne further established his Old Trafford legend by taking Sir Bobby Charlton's all-time club goalscoring record. Having already overtaken Sir Bobby's scoring record for England – subsequently held by Harry Kane – Wazza moved into an outright lead with his 250th Reds goal in January 2017.

Typically, it was scored in spectacular fashion, saving a draw for United at Stoke with a staggering top-corner free-kick.

Rooney's return to Everton in the summer of 2017 brought one of the truly great Old Trafford careers to an end, with Wayne claiming more honours than most and more goals than anyone, ever.

For any goalscorer pulling on the famous United shirt, Wayne Rooney is the all-time benchmark.

TROPHY HAUL

x5 Premier League: 2006/07, 2007/08, 2008/09, 2010/11, 2012/13

x1 Champions League: 2008

x1 FA Cup: 2016

x4 League Cup: 2006, 2009, 2010, 2017

x4 Community Shield: 2007, 2010, 2011, 2016

x1 Europa League: 2017

x1 Club World Cup: 2008

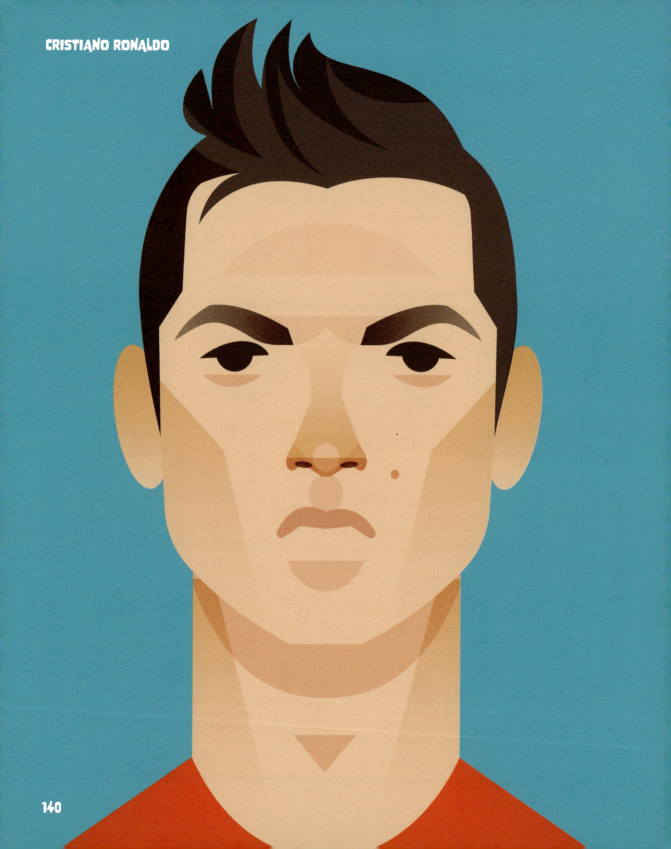

'THE GOAT'
CRISTIANO RONALDO

The Greatest Of All Time? He's one of our four *Ballon d'Or* winners, and a player that thrilled Old Trafford in two separate spells at either end of his career...

For many, he's the GOAT. But, while debate will forever rage about his comparisons to Messi, Maradona, Pele and others, Cristiano Ronaldo is unquestionably one of the finest footballers ever to grace Old Trafford and, thankfully, we were able to enjoy his brilliance in two separate spells.

United were aware of a gifted young Portuguese winger on Sporting Lisbon's books long before a pre-season friendly between the two clubs in August 2003, but the 18-year-old's display that evening convinced Sir Alex Ferguson that he had to be signed there and then.

Sporting won 3-1, United were tattered by young Ronaldo and the United boss insisted

When he won the Ballon d'Or in 2008, Ronaldo began a decade-long period of himself and Lionel Messi taking the prize every year (five each).

Cristiano is the joint record winner (with David De Gea) of the Sir Matt Busby Player of the Year award — he won it four times.

Cristiano's success has made him world famous, but he is most beloved in his homeland of Madeira, where visitors land at the Cristiano Ronaldo International Airport and can also visit the official CR7 museum in Funchal.

Ronaldo's finest season for the Reds came in 2007/08 when he scored 42 goals in 49 appearances!

CRISTIANO RONALDO

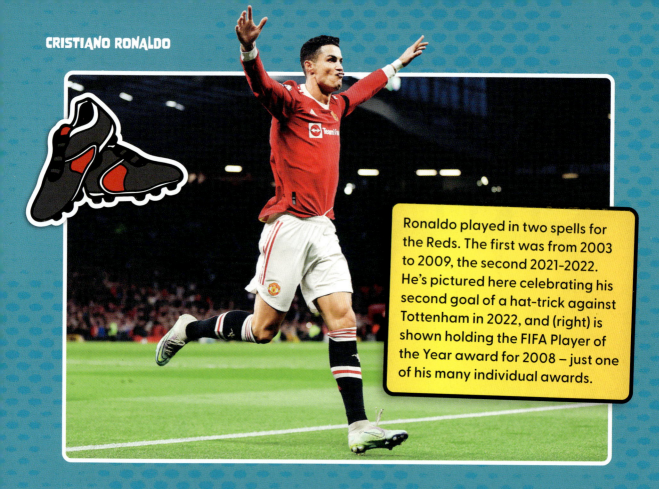

Ronaldo played in two spells for the Reds. The first was from 2003 to 2009, the second 2021-2022. He's pictured here celebrating his second goal of a hat-trick against Tottenham in 2022, and (right) is shown holding the FIFA Player of the Year award for 2008 – just one of his many individual awards.

that he and his squad weren't leaving the stadium until a deal had been done. As such, everything was agreed straight after the game, while the United players were sat waiting on the team coach, and Cristiano was over in England just days later to replace David Beckham as the Reds' new no.7!

He didn't start United's first game of the season, at home to Bolton, but he entered as a second-half substitute and absolutely stole the show. A narrow 1-0 lead at the time of his introduction evolved into a 4-0 romp by full-time.

"A marvellous debut, almost unbelievable," grinned Sir Alex, while Reds legend George Best labelled it: "Undoubtedly the most exciting debut performance I've ever seen."

Having made a brilliant first impression, Ronaldo continued to develop as he adapted to the physicality of the Premier League. He ended his first season at the club by starring in the FA Cup final, opening the scoring as United beat Millwall 3-0 and, although he had a tough time in 2004/05 and had to search for his best form, he ended 2005/06 in peak condition. Having grown physically and emotionally, he was ready to show the world how good he could be and so, in 2006/07, he announced himself as one

CRISTIANO RONALDO

FRED'S FACTS!

346
This appearance total came from two spells, with his most-faced opponents being Arsenal (18 games).

145
Tottenham suffered most from Ronaldo's sublime finishing, with 10 of this goal tally coming against them.

210
This figure is not a mistake – Cristiano really had played this many times for Portugal by the end of 2023/24, scoring 130 goals... and these crazy numbers were still set to go higher!

of the best players on the planet. Having hit 27 goals in his first three seasons combined, he notched 23 in '06/07 alone, a superb figure for a player still spending most of his time on the wing. The fastest feet in world football were a driving force as United reclaimed the Premier League title for the first time since 2002/03, and Cristiano became – often literally – central to a new era of dominance.

Ronaldo was increasingly used through the middle as a striker, and in 2007/08 he hit a mind-blowing 42 goals in 49 games as the Reds won a Premier League and Champions League Double, adding the Club World Cup months later to be crowned the best team on the planet. By that point, Cristiano had also won his first *Ballon d'Or* (one of five in total!), and Real Madrid began seriously pushing to sign him. United were aware of his dream to one day represent the Spanish giants, and resisted as long as possible before

CRISTIANO RONALDO

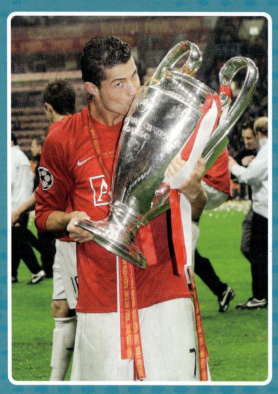

agreeing a world record £80 million transfer in the summer of 2009.

Cristiano continued to shatter records, winning countless honours with Real over the course of nine seasons there, and he remained beloved at Old Trafford – despite scoring home and away against the Reds in the 2012/13 Champions League! Rumours frequently surfaced that he could one day return, and that day finally came in August 2021.

Despite being in his late thirties, his goalscoring abilities remained unchanged by time, and he added another 27 goals in 54 outings before departing again in 2023. At the time of his leaving, a club statement thanked him for 'his immense contribution across two spells at Old Trafford'. There can be no better summary for the United career of one of the all-time greats.

TROPHY HAUL

x3
Premier League:
2006/07,
2007/08,
2008/09

x1
FA Cup:
2004

x2
League Cup:
2006,
2009

x1
Community Shield:
2007

x1
Champions League:
2008

x1
Club World Cup:
2008

CRISTIANO RONALDO

MAGIC MOMENT

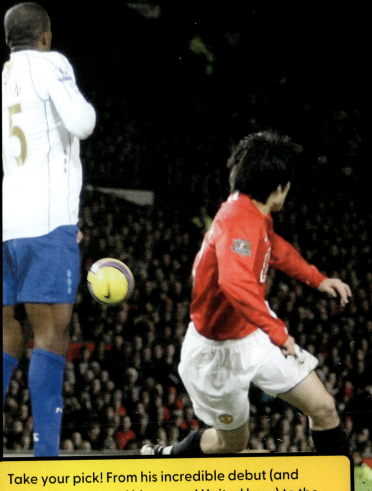

Take your pick! From his incredible debut (and the fanfare around his second United bow) to the countless major honours he won with the Reds, there are so many. The one clip used to illustrate his brilliance more than any other, though, is his ludicrous top-corner free-kick against Portsmouth in 2008 – a goal he called a "Ronaldo rocket"!

'THE GUNNER'
JACK ROWLEY

Meet the man whose explosive shots earned him his nickname – a forward who starred for Sir Matt Busby's first amazing team in the late '40s and early '50s…

If you go on the United website or app and look at the list of players in the top 10 of our all-time goalscorers list, there are many legendary names who are instantly recognisable, even to young fans. Wayne Rooney, Bobby Charlton, Denis Law, George Best… some of the most famous footballers ever! But there are also some other names which younger supporters might not have heard of, but who have still played a massive part in the club's history. And that is one of the reasons for this book – to educate younger supporters about the brilliance of players such as Jack Rowley, who was one of United's greatest-ever centre-forwards. And what a story it is…

Jack netted 12 hat-tricks for United, with only Denis Law claiming the matchball more times (18) for the Reds!

Rowley was a hugely popular player among United fans but was also one of Sir Alex Ferguson's favourite-ever footballers.

After hanging up his boots as a player, Jack went into management, taking charge of six clubs including Plymouth, Ajax, and Wrexham.

Jack was a soldier during the Second World War and was involved in the liberation of France – known as the Normandy landings – in June 1944.

JACK ROWLEY

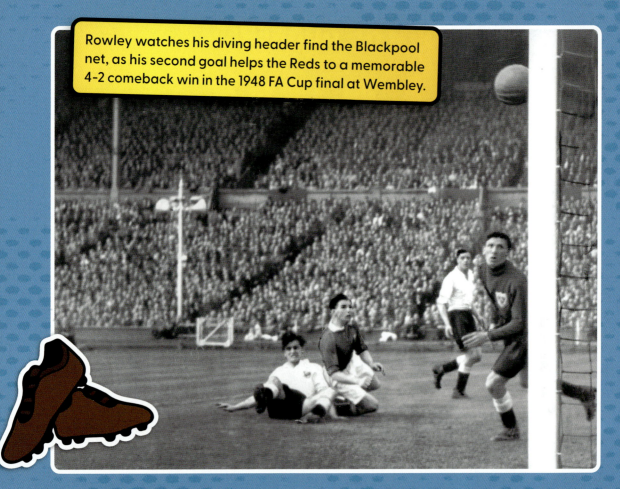

Rowley watches his diving header find the Blackpool net, as his second goal helps the Reds to a memorable 4-2 comeback win in the 1948 FA Cup final at Wembley.

Rowley was a legendary figure in Sir Matt Busby's first great United side and played a huge role in delivering trophies back to Old Trafford after a very difficult period. In fact, when Jack signed for United from Bournemouth while still a teenager, in 1937, the Reds were in the Second Division – can you imagine that? In his first season his goals helped United to finish second in Division Two to gain promotion back to the top flight. Disaster was soon to strike, though – with the outbreak of the Second World War, football was halted for six full seasons, robbing many players, including Jack, of the best years of their career as they joined the Army and were sent off to fight in the conflict.

When the war ended and league football finally returned in 1946/47, United had a new manager in Matt Busby. Jack and his team-mates were desperate to make up for lost time and reached the FA Cup final in 1948 where they were to face Blackpool, one of England's best teams at the time. Twice Blackpool took

JACK ROWLEY

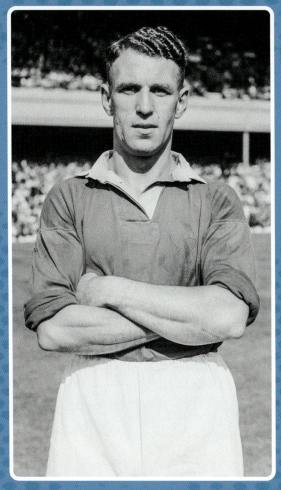

FRED'S FACTS!

424
Rowley racked up this many United games in an era without European football or the League Cup.

211
Gunner blasted a double-century of goals for the Reds, with only Rooney, Charlton and Law scoring more.

6
Jack's half-dozen games for England brought him six goals... and questions about why he didn't play more!

the lead, but Rowley twice scored to draw United level, with the Reds going on to win 4-2 in front of 100,000 fans to secure the first of Busby's many trophies.

It was to be a glorious period for Rowley who had developed into one of England's best strikers, but despite that, he was only selected six times for the international team – scoring six goals in those matches. England must have had loads of brilliant forwards to choose from if they could overlook that goal ratio! With the FA Cup in the trophy cabinet, the next aim was

JACK ROWLEY

becoming champions of England again. And, having come so close, with United finishing second in four of Busby's first five seasons in charge, finally the league title was won for the first time in over four decades in 1951/52 – Rowley finishing as top scorer in the division with a highly impressive 30 goals.

The Rowley family would no doubt have been proud of Jack's footballing achievements, but they had even more to be proud of. Believe it or not, Jack's little brother Arthur scored even more goals in his professional career! Arthur still holds the record for scoring the most goals of any player in the history of the Football League – an incredible 434 goals! So between them, the Rowley brothers – who were both nicknamed 'Gunner' for their powerful, cannon-like

TROPHY HAUL

First Division: x1 — 1951/52
FA Cup: x1 — 1948
Charity Shield: x1 — 1952

JACK ROWLEY

MAGIC MOMENT

A hat-trick against Arsenal in April 1952 helped clinch a first league title for the Reds in 41 years. On the brink of sealing the championship, Rowley (second from left, second row) scored after eight minutes, and twice again in the second half, as United won 6-1.

shooting ability – scored 642 goals just in league matches... wow!

Jack's United career came to an end in 1955 as the brilliant young Busby Babes emerged – leaving to become player-manager of Plymouth Argyle – but he left as a legend. He is one of only five players for United to have scored five or more goals in a single game, getting five in our 8-0 win over Yeovil Town in the FA Cup in 1949 (the others being Dimitar Berbatov, Andy Cole, George Best and Harold Halse) and only Rooney, Charlton and Law have scored more goals for the club. But just imagine how many he may have scored had he not lost six years to war – he might have been our greatest-ever goalscorer...

'THE GREAT DANE'
PETER SCHMEICHEL

An era-defining stopper for both club and country, this giant between the sticks wore the gloves through some of the Reds' most historic moments...

United have been lucky to have some amazing goalkeepers, but not many of them have been as good as 'the Great Dane' Peter Schmeichel. At 6ft 4in tall, the Denmark-born netminder towered over most team-mates and opponents and was regarded by many as the best keeper in the world during the '90s – only matched by Germany no.1 Oliver Kahn.

He was the Reds' goalkeeper through some of the club's most successful years and many say he's the greatest player to ever guard our net, with his crowning achievement being his crucial role in his unforgettable final season.

Peter was born in Gladsaxe, Denmark, in 1963 and played for Gladsaxe-Hero, Hvidovre and Brondby on his way to representing his

Peter has the second-most clean sheets in United's history (180), behind only David De Gea (190).

Schmeichel has a surprisingly strong goalscoring record for a keeper – he scored for United, Aston Villa and Denmark!

His son, Kasper Schmeichel, is also a famous goalkeeper who won the Premier League with Leicester City.

Peter was part of the 1992 Euros success achieved by Denmark, keeping a clean sheet in the final against Germany.

PETER SCHMEICHEL

The Great Dane was as animated as they come and a very vocal presence as our last line of defence, often using his imposing frame to repel attacks, a strategy that helped us lift a load of trophies, including five Premier League titles (right).

country. He made his international debut in May 1988, and was so good that his performances brought him to the attention of a lot of big clubs, including United. So impressed was Alex Ferguson by Schmeichel that he moved quickly to sign him as a Red in August 1991 for £500,000, in what turned out to be one of the club's best ever transfers.

Within a few months of his debut season of 1991/92, it was clear the Reds had got a world-class keeper. He helped the side win the League Cup, but the main aim of winning the First Division title slipped agonisingly away in the final games of the season. Not to worry, though; Peter and the Reds quickly made amends in 1992/93, at the beginning of the Premier League era. While the new competition started slowly for United, by the end of the campaign Ferguson's side were crowned champions of England.

The Dane's part in the success? Countless acrobatic saves, a liking for rushing off

PETER SCHMEICHEL

FRED'S FACTS!

398
Schmeichel averaged roughly 50 games a season across his eight campaigns with the Reds.

1
This is Peter's goal tally for the Reds – yes, really! – after he scored a header against Rotor Volgograd at Old Trafford in September 1995!

129
His Denmark cap count (with 51 clean sheets) includes his part in his country's Euros '92 success.

his line to block with any part of his body, and long throws to launch wingers Ryan Giggs and Andrei Kanchelskis on lightning counterattacks. He was a goalkeeper unlike any that Reds fans had seen before.

Having helped end United's 26-year wait for a league title, Schmeichel then helped the Reds to further glory. With Steve Bruce and Gary Pallister in front of him, Peter helped create one of the strongest defensive triangles ever seen in English football. So high were their standards that they'd often be seen shouting at each other, almost as if they were angry. Except this was simply their way of geeing each other up, of staying alert to the threat of the opposition attackers. And guess what? It worked! United were Premier League champions again in 1993/94 and even added the FA Cup, to give the club its first ever league and cup Double.

The team changed a lot over the next two seasons, with a wave of youngsters

PETER SCHMEICHEL

MAGIC MOMENT

When United gave away a penalty in the last minute of our FA Cup semi-final replay against Arsenal in April 1999, it felt like our season might be taking a downward turn. Dennis Bergkamp stepped up, but he couldn't find a way past the Great Dane, who dived to his left to palm away the spot-kick. In extra-time, Giggs won us the tie, but without that Schmeichel save United probably wouldn't have won the Treble.

– like David Beckham and Paul Scholes – replacing established stars. Against the odds, in 1995/96 the Reds did the Double again, and claimed the league again in 1996/97. For Peter, that was his fourth league title in six seasons.

His defensive unit with Bruce and Pallister had broken up by 1997/98, with both centre-backs departing the club, and a season that started so well fell away as Arsenal collected their own Double.

Experts predicted the Gunners were now set for a period of dominance, but United were having none of it. In his final season as a Red – having decided to leave due to fatigue caused by English football's hectic schedule – he signed off by winning the lot! No team had ever won the Treble when

United achieved the feat in the 1998/99 season, and Schmeichel was at the forefront of all three trophy wins. In the Premier League he missed just four games, reaching double figures for clean sheets, as he won his fifth English title. Next, Newcastle were beaten in the FA Cup final – a 2-0 win at Wembley.

Then came the showstopper, the Champions League final against Bayern Munich. With usual captain Roy Keane suspended, Schmeichel – no stranger to barking orders – was given the armband. Two dramatic injury-time goals from Teddy Sheringham and Ole Gunnar Solskjaer gave the Reds a 2-1 victory for the final piece of the Treble (right).

Even before this incredible ending, the Dane had long since been assured of his lofty place in Manchester United's history – but what a way to bow out!

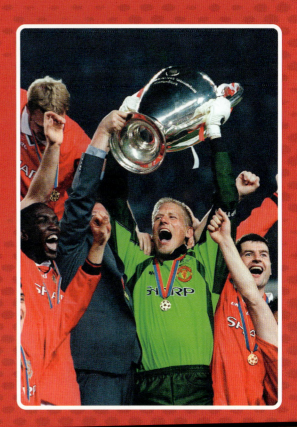

TROPHY HAUL

 **x5** Premier League: 1992/93, 1993/94, 1995/96, 1996/97, 1998/99

 **x3** FA Cup: 1994, 1996, 1999

 x1 League Cup: 1992

 x4 Charity Shield: 1993, 1994, 1996, 1997

 **x1** Champions League: 1999

 **x1** European Super Cup: 1991

'THE MIDFIELD MAESTRO'
PAUL SCHOLES

This creative genius was a member of United's 'Class of '92' youth team and a key part of Sir Alex Ferguson's two Champions League-winning sides...

Paul Scholes had many affectionate nicknames as a footballer: from 'the Ginger Ninja' to the more predictable 'Scholesy', which lots of people still call him today. Another fans' favourite was 'Sat-Nav'... because he always knew the right direction to find a fellow Red when the ball was at his feet. Indeed, one of Scholes's favourite tricks on the training ground was striking a football hard at a team-mate's backside from 40 yards away!

Thankfully, he was just as precise in proper matches. He played an incredible 718 games for us between 1994-2013 – only Ryan Giggs and Sir Bobby Charlton have played more – and ranks 10th on our all-time scorers list with 155 goals. Not bad for a midfielder!

Scholes loved a tackle – and he'd be the first to admit he didn't always time them right! In the Premier League he picked up 97 yellow cards.

As a youngster Paul was a striker, but he played the majority of his career at United in the position he is renowned for, in midfield.

Paul played for United's 1999 and 2008 Champions League winners, meaning he's ideally placed to assess which team was better. He picks the '99 lads, saying: "We just went out to score more than the other team!"

Scholes was never a fan of media duties as a player but can these days be found doing regular TV punditry!

PAUL SCHOLES

As a kid, Scholes was brilliant at cricket as well as football, but there was only ever going to be one winner after a United scout spotted him in action. Aged 14, Paul started training with the Reds, and he'd soon team up with a group of lads that would go on to win the FA Youth Cup in 1992, before many of them progressed to win more silverware (and we mean loads of it!) in the first team under Sir Alex Ferguson.

Scholes was also asthmatic, but he never let that hold him back, with his inhaler always nearby. "It was just something I had to live with, and take the medication," he once said. His first-team debut came in September 1994, when we beat Port Vale 2-1 in the League Cup. He scored both goals – what a start!

While there were faster players and better dribblers in the team, Scholes's intelligence and passing would make him such a key player for both United and England in the years that followed, with even the biggest legends in the game

> Two down, one to go: Paul holds tightly to the FA Cup after United have beaten Newcastle in the 1999 final, as the Reds march towards the Treble. He scored in that Cup final, but it's his stunning volley at Aston Villa in December 2006 (above, right) that is often picked out as the finest of his many great goals for United.

PAUL SCHOLES

FRED'S FACTS!

718
Scholesy's impressive number of appearances came in nine different competitions. Amazing!

155
There was every type of goal in Paul's sizeable tally, but mostly they were spectacular.

66
Scholes retired from international football aged 29, but only after winning 66 England caps and scoring 14 goals.

picking Paul out as their toughest ever opponent. "Scholes is undoubtedly the greatest midfielder of his generation – I would have loved to have played alongside him," said Zinedine Zidane. Xavi and Thierry Henry are two other world-class stars of that time who named Scholes as the best midfielder they ever faced, but our no.18 was never one to let such praise go to his head. He preferred to dodge the spotlight, and he did his best to avoid interviews – although, as you'll know if you've seen him on TV as a pundit, he's a bit more comfortable in front of the camera these days! In 2004, when Paul was 29, he was asked to share his 'perfect day'. His response? "Train in the morning. Pick up my children from school. Play with them. Have tea. Put them to bed and then watch a bit of TV."

Such a professional and humble attitude to his job helped him achieve so much success, as he won 11 Premier League titles, as well as three FA Cups, two League Cups and two Champions Leagues – including one to complete our historic Treble in 1998/99. Sadly, Scholes missed the '99 final against Bayern Munich through suspension, but he'd be in the starting XI when we beat Chelsea in the final in Moscow in 2008. He didn't score against the London side that night, but he did net six times against the Blues – all tidy finishes, as you'd expect with Scholes, but not on the same level as some of his long-range rockets that we could watch all day long. There was his volley, straight from a corner, away to Bradford City in 2000, which team-mate Dwight Yorke wisely ducked out the way of! Then there's the rifled winner against Barcelona in the 2007/08 Champions League semi-final second leg – probably his most important goal. But you can't look beyond his thunderbolt away to Aston Villa in 2006 as the ultimate Scholesy smash, as he met a ball dropping from the skies outside the

TROPHY HAUL

x11 Premier League: 1995/96, 1996/97, 1998/99, 1999/2000, 2000/01, 2002/03, 2006/07, 2007/08, 2008/09, 2010/11, 2012/13

x2 Champions League: 1999, 2008

x3 FA Cup: 1996, 1999, 2004

x2 League Cup: 2009, 2010

x1 Club World Cup: 2008

x1 Intercontinental Cup: 1999

x5 Charity/Community Shield: 1996, 1997, 2003, 2008, 2010

PAUL SCHOLES

MAGIC MOMENT

We're spoilt for choice with options for his finest moment, but his stunning swerving strike in the 2008 Champions League semi-final against Barcelona really does take some beating (and it took us to the Moscow final!). Of all the vital goals he created and scored, this one comes top of the pile every time.

area to volley it home via the underside of the crossbar. What a goal!

It was a sad day when he finally retired in May 2011, but incredibly he'd be back six months later, when he stepped up in an injury crisis to help Sir Alex out. Now wearing the no.22 shirt (Ashley Young had adopted his favourite no.18!) Scholes would play a further 41 games before retiring – for real this time – in May 2013, at the same time Sir Alex departed as United boss. Legends, both.

'THE TOOTHLESS TIGER'

NOBBY STILES

The extraordinary story of how a tough young lad from north Manchester rose through United's youth ranks to become one of the Reds' most-loved players...

Nobby was nicknamed 'El Bandito' by newspapers in Argentina because of his aggressive tackling style!

Despite his receding hair and missing teeth, Nobby was once voted the world's most popular man by readers of a women's magazine!

Only two English footballers have played in victorious World Cup and Champions League finals (or European Cup, as it used to be called), and both of them represented Manchester United. You might be able to guess one of them: Sir Bobby Charlton, who sadly passed away in October 2023. Sir Bobby was one of the greatest footballers of all time; maybe even the greatest English player ever. But the second person, Norbert Stiles, is not quite as famous. Maybe the shorter version of his name – 'Nobby' – might ring a bell! If you know that song that England fans sing, *Three Lions*, you may have noticed his name pop up in the lyrics. There's a bit that goes '*Bobby belting the ball... and*

Stiles was a youth-team coach at United from 1989-1993, working with the likes of Ryan Giggs, David Beckham and Paul Scholes.

Nobby was a devout Catholic all through his life, and during the 1966 World Cup he went to mass every day!

NOBBY STILES

World Cup winners: Stiles shares a (toothless) smile with manager Alf Ramsey and captain Bobby Moore after England beat West Germany in the 1966 final at Wembley.

Nobby dancing!' That bit is included because when England beat West Germany to win the World Cup in 1966, Nobby was so excited that he started dancing on the Wembley pitch during the celebrations! That was the kind of character he was when the final whistle went: fun and down to earth.

He was born in Collyhurst, north Manchester and grew up idolising the Busby Babes – the amazing United team of the 1950s, which was full of young, skilful players. Eventually, he was spotted by our scouts and invited to train and help the ground staff at Old Trafford. Football was very different back then – Nobby's first wage at United was £3.25 a week! He impressed everyone with his skills and was eventually taken on as a professional in 1958, but that was also the year of the Munich Air Disaster, when eight United players were killed in a plane crash. Those players were Nobby's heroes and the tragedy really affected him. He was at Old Trafford when the news came through, and was sent home early.

He made his debut for the first team against Bolton in October 1960 and

NOBBY STILES

scored his first goal a few weeks later, in a 3-2 win against Newcastle. Nobby was just 18 when he got into the first team, though his first few seasons were a little up and down.

But by 1964/65, he was one of the regulars in Matt Busby's team. And that was the season we won our first league title since before Munich. This new team was loved by fans because it was so attacking, so exciting, with amazing players like George Best, Denis Law and, of course, Bobby Charlton. Nobby was skilful but a more defensive player, and he took part in 59 of our 60 games that season – as many as George and Bobby.

Nobby was brilliant at tackling. He was only 5ft 6in, with two front teeth missing and very poor eyesight (which meant he had to wear contact lenses on the pitch), but there was nobody tougher. His team-mates jokingly called him

FRED'S FACTS!

395
This appearance tally places Nobby in United's all-time top 50 – in 32nd place to be precise!

19
Stiles took most pleasure from snuffing out the opposition but still managed to weigh in with goals.

28
He represented England this many times, most famously in the 1966 World Cup finals.

NOBBY STILES

'Happy' because he was so ferocious and determined on the pitch. He would always stand up for himself and United's other players, and loved a battle. When England won the 1966 World Cup, they played Portugal in the semi-finals. They had a striker called Eusebio, who was one of the best players in the world at the time. He won the Golden Boot for scoring nine times in the tournament, but Nobby man-marked him and didn't give him a sniff as England won 2-0. The whole country fell in love with Stiles, calling him 'The Toothless Tiger' because he had to leave his false teeth in the dressing room!

Winning the World Cup was the highlight of Stiles's career, along with the 1968 European Cup final. Like in 1966, Nobby was given the job of tracking Eusebio, Benfica's star player. Nobby

TROPHY HAUL

x2 First Division: 1964/65, 1966/67

x1 European Cup: 1968

x1 FA Cup: 1963

x2 Charity Shield: 1965 (shared), 1967 (shared)

x1 World Cup: 1966

NOBBY STILES

MAGIC MOMENT

Nobby was remembered for his part in England's World Cup win in 1966, nullifying Portugal's main man Eusebio in the semi-final. He was given the same role again in the European Cup against Benfica at Wembley in May 1968, keeping his rival quiet once more as the Reds became England's first continental champions.

was getting more injury problems by this time – he only played 28 matches in 1967/68 – but he did a near-perfect job again. United won 4-1 to become kings of Europe, and Nobby was one of eight Academy players in the Reds' 12-man squad at Wembley.

Sadly, Nobby's injury problems meant he played just 32 times in his last two seasons at Old Trafford. He left to join Middlesbrough and then Preston, where he later became a manager. He returned to United and helped to coach the youth team in the 1990s, but he sadly passed away in 2020. He will always be much loved as a legend of England and United, for his incredible achievements but also his wonderful personality.

'THE LOCAL GIRL'
ELLA TOONE

Years after 'Rooo-ney' could be heard ringing around Old Trafford, in 2018 a new United chant was created – as the fans celebrated a new hero… 'Tooo-ney!'

From the first time she kicked a football in the garden of her family home in Tyldesley, just a few miles up the road from United Women's Leigh Sports Village home, Ella Toone looked born to play for the Reds. At the age of just seven, in 2007, she did just that, when she joined the club's 'Centre of Excellence', a programme that aimed to develop talented local girls to help give them the chance of playing at the highest level.

With United not having a senior women's team at that time, Ella made the move to Blackburn Rovers in 2015 as she approached her late teens, before she spent two years with Manchester City. But the team she really wanted to line up for played in red, and when a professional United team was set up in 2018,

Ella loved all sports when she was in primary school, and won awards at gymnastics – something which proves handy for goal celebrations!

In January 2024, Ella was named in FIFA's Women's World XI, voted for by 28,000 professional footballers, joining her United team-mate at the time, Mary Earps. What an achievement!

As well as representing England, Ella appeared at the 2020 Tokyo olympics for Great Britain, joining the action against Chile.

Toone's idol growing up was Cristiano Ronaldo – with CR7 first joining United when Ella was three years old. "I always wore his boots and his no.7 growing up," she has said.

ELLA TOONE

Whether a scorer or creator, for United or England, Ella is always playing a key role, working just as hard in training (above, right) as she does in matches.

Ella was so happy to get the call from the club she loved the most, as one of seven players to return having previously played for the Reds at youth level.

Toone was handed the iconic no.7 shirt worn by so many Reds legends throughout our history – as seen in this book! – and came on as a half-time sub in United Women's first-ever professional match: a 1-0 win at Liverpool in August 2018. It didn't take Ella long to find her groove, ending that first season with 15 goals from 29 games in all competitions as United roared to the Championship title and promotion to the WSL.

As either a forward or a midfielder, Ella brings so much attacking threat to whatever team she plays in, with her brilliant range of passing seeing her rack up almost as many assists as goals since that first season back at the club. The United fans watching on in the stands or on TV love Ella's work ethic and passion just as much as her quality on the ball.

Ahead of the 2024/25 season, no player had played more games, or scored more

ELLA TOONE

FRED'S FACTS!

164
Number of games played for United up until the end of the 2023/24 season – a team record.

53
Ella's goals return is also a United Women record – she's twice got into double figures in a single season.

2007
In the years after she first joined our Centre of Excellence she got to meet many of her United heroes. Check out this pic of Ella with Rio!

goals, for United Women than 'Tooney' – to use her catchy nickname – with so many amazing moments along the way.

There's the time she scored five goals in one game against Leicester in the 2019/20 League Cup; her far-post finish away to Arsenal in November 2022 as we fought back for a famous win in front of 40,000 fans; and (best of all) her FA Cup final cracker that won United Women's Goal of the Season prize for 2023/24 – a 30-yard screamer that gave the Tottenham goalie no chance, setting us up for a 4-0 triumph.

While Toone has twice been voted United Women Player of the Year, as well as sharing the Players' Player award with Maya Le Tissier in 2023/24, that 2023/24 season was also special for the manner of Ella's nine goals, with

ELLA TOONE

MAGIC MOMENT

It has to be her wondergoal in the 2024 Women's FA Cup final. In first-half injury-time, Ella charged forward with the ball into the Tottenham half, before cutting onto her right foot while squeezing between two opponents, and unleashing a delicious finish to break the Wembley deadlock. Wow!

ELLA TOONE

that Cup final strike against Spurs being one of so many long-range rockets from her lethal right boot.

She's scored some worldies for England too, of course, famously being the Lionesses' super-sub in both the quarter-final and final of Euro 2022, scoring a vital goal each time as England won the trophy. Her amazing, chipped finish in the final against Germany made her a household name way beyond the north-west of England, which she's admitted took a little getting used to!

Fame hasn't changed Tooney one bit though, and after starting up a popular podcast with her best mate (and former United team-mate) Alessia Russo, Ella's humour and down-to-earth attitude makes for great entertainment, while proving that she'll always be a Greater Manchester girl at heart!

x1 — Women's Championship: 2018/19

x1 — Women's FA Cup: 2024

x1 — European Championship: 2022

'THE CALMEST OF KEEPERS'

EDWIN VAN DER SAR

This legendary Dutch keeper didn't join United until the age of 34, but that didn't stop him becoming a key figure in Sir Alex Ferguson's third great United side...

Whenever Edwin van der Sar was in Manchester United's goal, you had a strong feeling of comfort. It didn't matter if there was a long shot, a header, a one-on-one or even a stray backpass to be dealt with, you knew the big Dutchman would sort it out. And he did that for six fantastic years, from 2005-2011, acting as the base of a team that became champions of England, Europe and the world.

Van der Sar had been the great goalkeeper of a successful Ajax team who had won the 1995 Champions League. He was tall and muscular, but also thin and agile. He had good reflexes, caught crosses, barked at his defence to keep them organised and could pass with

Edwin saved three consecutive penalties in the 2007 Community Shield (against Chelsea), which is a very rare achievement!

Van der Sar played more games for the Netherlands national team than anyone else (130) until Wesley Sneijder overtook him in 2017.

Van der Sar set a world record in 2009 when he didn't concede a league goal for 1,311 minutes.

Edwin became the oldest player to win the Premier League title when he kept goal for us in 2010/11 — he was 40 years and 205 days by the season's end.

EDWIN VAN DER SAR

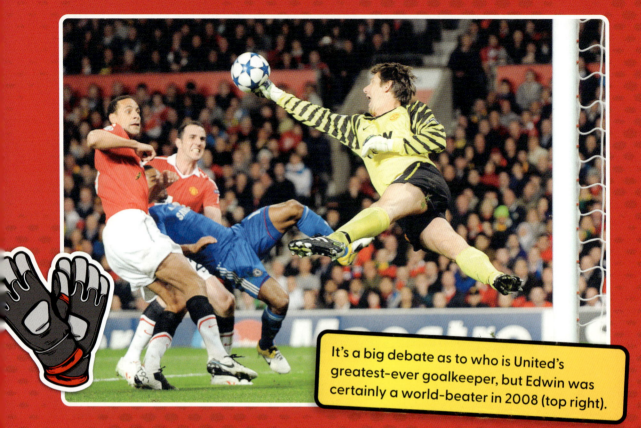

It's a big debate as to who is United's greatest-ever goalkeeper, but Edwin was certainly a world-beater in 2008 (top right).

both feet. He was one of a new style of goalkeeper who sometimes came out of his box to clear the danger, almost like an extra defender.

It was this combination of abilities – combined with a cool, calm presence – that brought him to the attention of Sir Alex Ferguson, who first wanted to sign him in 1999. But Edwin joined Juventus and then Fulham, meaning it wasn't until 2005, when he was aged 34, that he finally became a Red.

The team he joined was made up of exciting young talents like Wayne Rooney and Cristiano Ronaldo. And as an older player of vast experience, van der Sar was respected by everyone and they felt comfortable playing in front of him. This young side soon became Sir Alex's third great team – following the 1993-1994 Premier League winners, and then the Treble-winners of 1999.

This new side – with Rio Ferdinand and Nemanja Vidic in defence, Paul Scholes and Michael Carrick in midfield – won their first Premier League together in 2007 and looked ready to compete for the ultimate trophy in club football. His part in achieving that was crucial.

The 2007/08 season started with the Community Shield against Chelsea at Wembley. After a 1-1 draw across 90

EDWIN VAN DER SAR

FRED'S FACTS!

266
Sir Alex Ferguson would have loved to have signed Edwin earlier but he still played this many games.

135
Number of clean sheets the Dutchman kept for the Reds – that's more than half of the matches he played in!

130
Van der Sar ranks second for all-time appearances for the Netherlands, and he finished fourth in the 1998 World Cup.

minutes, Edwin saved three penalties in a row in the shoot-out. It was an incredible display of goalkeeping to deny our biggest rivals in England and Europe… and it would be repeated!

Over the next 10 months, the two clubs fought it out for every trophy. Van der Sar helped United to win another Premier League, just like the year before, by keeping 15 clean sheets. It had also been a great season in Europe for Edwin – he conceded only three goals in nine games, helping United to set up a historic match against Chelsea in the Champions League final in Moscow.

Just like at Wembley at the start of the season, this match ended in a 1-1 draw, meaning another penalty shoot-out. Van der Sar was the hero once again. With the score level at 5-5, Nicolas Anelka stepped up for Chelsea. His shot was well struck, but Edwin guessed correctly and dived to his right, pushing away the effort

EDWIN VAN DER SAR

MAGIC MOMENT

Goalkeepers don't often get to celebrate like strikers, but his shoot-out save from Nicolas Anelka in Moscow in May 2008 was Edwin's moment. His team-mates sprinted from the halfway line to join him in a celebratory huddle in Moscow's Luzhniki Stadium. And why not, United has just won the Champions League thanks to his amazing save. "The greatest moment of your life" is how he later described it.

EDWIN VAN DER SAR

and then roaring in celebration as his United team-mates piled on top of him.

Edwin remained at his best the next season, breaking lots of records. First, he achieved the longest run of clean sheets in Premier League history, then in English history, then eventually in the entire history of world football. His reward? A third successive Premier League title. United were also crowned FIFA Club World Cup champions in December 2008, defeating Ecuador's LDU Quito 1-0 with 10 men in the final in Japan.

The Reds lost the Champions League final in 2008/09, and again two years later – both times against Barcelona. After the 2011 UCL final, van der Sar retired, aged nearly 41 years old. Those playing today still talk about watching Edwin and learning how to become the complete goalkeeper, because that's what he was across his whole career – and right until to the very end.

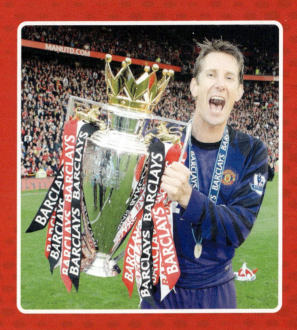

TROPHY HAUL

x4 Premier League: 2006/07, 2007/08, 2008/09, 2010/11

x1 Champions League: 2008

x2 League Cup: 2006, 2010

x3 Charity Shield: 2007, 2008, 2010

x1 Club World Cup: 2008

'BIG NORM'
NORMAN WHITESIDE

Record-breaker Whiteside became United's youngest ever goalscorer, the youngest scorer in a domestic cup final, the youngest Red to 200 games, and the youngest to appear in a World Cup finals (for Northern Ireland in 1982).

Meet the Northern Irishman who quickly rose through the Reds' youth ranks to make his mark as a teenage big-game goal-getter...

If you ask fans of other clubs to name United legends from the past, Norman Whiteside might not come up that high on the list of players they remember. But ask anyone who stood and cheered at the top of their voices at Old Trafford week in, week out in the 1980s, and you'll quickly hear the name of 'Big Norm' mentioned.

After breaking into the first team as a forward at just 16 years old, this Northern Irish international's lethal shooting and powerful heading made him a key weapon in United's armoury. Later he would often revert to a deeper midfield role, where his all-action approach and habit of scoring important goals made him a feared opponent among the Reds' rivals.

Norman was brought to United by the same man who discovered George Best — legendary scout Bob Bishop. The Reds had to move quickly after hearing Liverpool were also hoping to sign him.

While playing for local teams as a youngster in his home town of Belfast, Norm once scored 10 goals in a game!

When he scored in both the 1983 League Cup final and the FA Cup final, Whiteside became the first man ever to score in both finals in the same season.

NORMAN WHITESIDE

After starting out as a striker for the Reds, he soon dropped back into midfield where he could put his physical approach to full use – such as here against Everton – often playing alongside his captain and good friend Bryan Robson (top right).

Norman is one of the most famous youth graduates in United's history. He made his debut for the club on 24 April 1982, aged only 16, in a 1-0 win away at Brighton & Hove Albion, becoming the youngest player to make the first team since the legendary Duncan Edwards in 1953.

Soon after, Northern Ireland manager Billy Bingham called him up to their World Cup squad for the 1982 finals in Spain, and when he returned for the 1982/83 season, then United boss Ron Atkinson decided, despite his youth, that Norman was ready to start up front for the Reds.

The youngster rewarded that faith with four goals in the first five games of the campaign, and when Atkinson's men reached both domestic cup finals that season, the Belfast-born teenager would play a huge role. His goal against Liverpool in the League Cup final couldn't prevent a 1-2 defeat for United, but his volleyed winner against Arsenal in the FA Cup semi-final sent Atkinson's side to Wembley again, and when the final against Brighton went to a replay, he headed home in a 4-0 win to become the youngest ever scorer in an FA Cup final.

NORMAN WHITESIDE

FRED'S FACTS!

274
Norman's appearance total for the Reds, with his busiest season being his 57 games in 1982/83.

67
He scored this many times for United, but it was the quality and timing of his goals that really stood out.

38
A surprise starter at the 1982 World Cup for Northern Ireland, he won this many caps for his country.

His reputation as big-game player against Liverpool – which made United supporters love him even more! – was boosted by other goals against the Merseysiders, such as his late equaliser at Anfield in January 1984 and winner there on Boxing Day 1986. A series of powerful displays in the middle of the park and up front also ensured that United frequently held their own against the team who were the dominant force in English football throughout the 1980s.

But it was his heroics against another club from the same city that would seal his place in United folklore. With 10 minutes of extra-time remaining in the 1985 FA Cup final against newly crowned league champions Everton, and with the Reds down to 10 men following a red card for centre-back Kevin Moran, Norman produced a moment of sheer magic.

He picked the ball up on the right wing, drove towards the Everton box, before curling a stunning shot inside the far post

NORMAN WHITESIDE

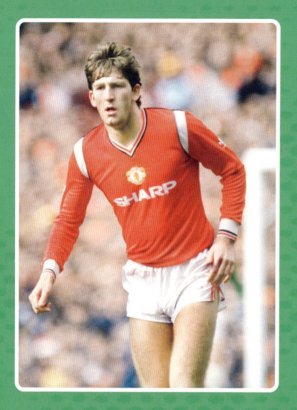

to seal a second FA Cup win in three years for United (below). The strike would later be voted Goal of the Season.

As the 1980s wore on, injury problems began to limit his appearances, and Norman would eventually move on to Everton, where 13 goals in his first season showed he still had much to offer. Sadly, further serious injury problems led to his retirement in 1991, aged only 26.

To this day, 'Big Norm' remains a true United legend, and is still a familiar face around Old Trafford on matchdays. He achieved a huge amount at a very young age and proved the old saying when anyone doubts if youth players should be given their chance at the highest level: "If they're good enough, they're old enough". Stormin' Norman was good enough – and so much more than that.

TROPHY HAUL

x2 FA Cup: 1983, 1985

x1 Charity Shield: 1983